# Night to Dawn

Marge Simon: pages 15, 33, and 46
Chris Friend: pages 3, 23, 44, and 84
Sandy DeLuca: front cover and pages 13, 29, 68, 74, and 86
Elizabeth Hattie Pierce-Collins: pages 20, 38, 79, and 99
Denny E. Marshall: back cover and pages 5, 25, 61, and 95

*Night to Dawn No. 44, October, 2023*, Copyright 2023 by Barbara Custer. All rights revert to individual author and artist after publication. ISSN # 1542-1430; ISBN: 978-1-937769-79-6
Night to Dawn is a semi-annual publication of fiction, poetry, artwork, articles, and review.
Orders, editorial, and queries: Barbara Custer, P. O. Box 643, Abington, PA 19001
Email: barbaracuster@hotmail.com or ntdsubmissions@gmail.com
PayPal orders: venus1021@juno.com.
Submissions: ntdsubmissions@gmail.com; Web: www.bloodredshadow.com

# Pickings and Tidbits

Top of the balloon to you! 😊

I'm contemplating Halloween—Tis the season, and my balloons would agree. So I used one of Sandy DeLuca's illustrations, which has a pumpkin, for the front cover. I will indulge in pumpkin-flavored coffee, pumpkin muffins, pumpkin Mylar balloons, and pumpkin ice cream, so in deference to The Great Pumpkin, I'm using an appropriate cover.

With that in mind, for *Night to Dawn 44*, I included horror-themed tales suited for Halloween. Starting with Lee Clark Zumpe, "The Quarantine Station" grabbed my attention. It reminded me of *The Island of Dr. Moreau*, except the mad scientist in Zumpe's tale experiments with raising the dead. On Facebook, I told people I wanted submissions based on the mummy theme. Rod Marsden came through with "An Unwrapping." Rajeev Bhargava submitted something which will appear in the next issue. His "Duppy" tale may connote cuteness until you meet the villain and his slew of casualties.

Ever had a boss you hated? A particular gutless one gets his comeuppance in Sharon Bidwell's "Brain Dead." Note to self: a zombie apocalypse is not the time to act like a jerk.

*Night to Dawn 44* ushers in a spot of humor with Ann Stolinsky's "SPU" and Christopher T. Dabrowski's "Transfer." The first jibes at inflation, and the latter features an interaction between a drunk and an angel who falls asleep on the job. I recommend you check out Stolinsky's bio. She's part owner of Gemini Wordsmiths, and she's a dynamite developmental editor.

Speaking of vampires and undead, tasty things do come "In Black Boxes," as Hillary Lyons reveals. In Hal Kempka's "Hunger Pangs," an old house is the vampire, feeding on families who dare try to live in it.

Sandy DeLuca did many illustrations for NTD 44; two of her poems are featured here. Likewise, so has Marge Simon, along with three prose pieces and two poems, bringing an enchanting flavor of the vampire genre, especially "La Citadel de Sangre." You'll see more work from Marge and Sandy in the next issue. I've artwork from Denny E. Marshall, whose back cover acknowledges my weakness for Mylar balloons. Chris Friend and Elizabeth Hattie Pierce also brought some striking illustrations to the party.

With each story in this issue, look for haunting poetry from Lee Clark Zumpe, Alexis Child, Marge Simon, Matthew Wilson, Denny E. Marshall, Hillary Lyon, and Todd Hanks.

Some good news: I'm currently editing Michael De Stefano's *The Bohemian* and hope to publish it in the early fall. I'd describe it as a mixture of romance and erotica. His other books, *The Gunslinger's Companion* and *Waiting for Grandfather*, have enjoyed excellent reviews, and I'm anticipating the same for his new release.

Some not-so-good news: Amazon KDP reported increased costs for paper and other supplies needed to manufacture books. Ergo, the prices for some of the NTD books have gone up. I will continue to offer *Night to Dawn* magazine for $7.50. However, in 2024, the retail cost for the magazine will go up to $7.99, but still $7.50 if you order off my website. I've been spending more time working on my WIP.

Here's an easy recipe for pumpkin cookies to help set the mood for Halloween. Ingredients: 2.5 cups flour, one teaspoon (tsp.) baking soda, one tsp. baking powder, one tsp.

cinnamon, 1.5 tsp. nutmeg, ½ tsp. salt, 1.5 cups sugar, one stick of butter, softened, one tsp. vanilla, one large egg, and one cup pumpkin puree. Preheat the oven to 350ᵒF, and grease your cookie pans. Combine flour, baking soda, baking powder, cinnamon, nutmeg, and salt in a medium bowl and sift. Beat sugar with butter in a large mixer bowl, then add pumpkin, egg, and vanilla extract. Gradually beat in the flour mixture. Drop by rounded tablespoon onto the baking sheets. Bake for 15 to 18 minutes until the edges are firm. Let them cool. For flavoring, you can drizzle icing over the cookies. Vanilla and pumpkin icing seem to work best.

In the meantime, I'm enjoying my pumpkin-flavored coffee and muffin with my dinner. I will go out and buy some pumpkin-shaped chocolates to give out for Halloween and try not to eat too many. ☺ I want to thank the authors, poets, and illustrators for sending me their work and the readers who enjoy the magazine. I appreciate all of you! ~~*Barbara of the Balloons*

# *Nosferatu, 2279 A.D.*
## *by*
## *Lee Clark Zumpe*

The Martian night crept into the room.

Motionless, Darren glared at the monitor.

Mist rolled across the tile, wispy fingers stretching with bold intent. Vapors crystallized, expanded, forged a tangible form. Hunger overpowered discretion. It struck hastily.

Incisors ripped synthetic skin, tore delicate circuitry.

The vampire choked on liquid coolant surging through the android's veins.

### *The End*

## Invocation by Lee Clark Zumpe

"Helpe then, O holy Virgin chiefe of nine,
Thy weaker Novice to performe thy will…"

*The First Booke of the Faerie Queen,* Proem ii.1, Edmund Spenser

Calliope, stir your soft voice for me:
Let it rain in whispers through fever dreams
To breathe sweet life into my poetry,
To invoke tone and images and themes;
Bless each word as if it was a frail child,
Give it sustenance and animation –
Make some of them strong, make some of them mild,
Provide each line proper derivation;
And word upon word, and line upon line,
Craft this society of language, muse,
Perfecting both devices and design,
Making my script with your intention fuse.

## Daughter of Monsters by Matthew Wilson

A boy summoning his courage
Valentine's candy for the new schoolgirl!
Her dark heart with no experience of kindness
Making her first gift to him a cure of his cancer.

# Brain Dead
## by
## Sharon Bidwell

1:05 p.m.

Teeth clamped hard, creating an agony of fire. Sarah gritted her jaw, refusing to scream. Sound would draw more trouble. Anger helped to render her silent even as her trait for survival kicked in, and she drove a knife into the creature's brainstem. As she fell gasping to the pavement, one fierce thought burned bright; more unpleasant than the sharp torment, pinching, and piercing flesh, was the knowledge of her impending death.

Since the outbreak, everyone had lived with the uncertainty, but the human optimistic heart always assumed eternal rest lay a way off, a future event. Brilliant sunshine, a limpid blue sky, didn't strike her as a terrific day to die. Upon waking, the sight had convinced her the change wouldn't happen this day. What a bummer to be proved wrong.

Silent shrieks smothered these thoughts, muffled her mind. Seconds ticked by, during which she fought the fight-or-flight reflex. Without hope for survival, there was no point in anything. Of even moving from this spot.

Untrue. Though inevitably dead, she still didn't want to be eaten. The damn things followed sound, but some detected fresh blood. Besides, no good came of sitting around, and she needed to do something important.

The corpse lay at her feet — inanimate, with the brainstem severed. Hard to recollect how she'd killed the creature, having slipped into madness.

Red. She'd seen red. Red blood. Red rage. Ruby as beetroot now in the face, simmering with adrenaline. Red-blooded in strength, powered by fear and anger. She'd shown the zombie a red card, crossed him out with red ink, a deficit being, a liability to the living. Run through a red light to kill the already-dead in self-defence; she was this creature's red meat. No rules of propriety applied any longer; no such thing as red-tape tethered actions. The red-hot poker in her arm said so, but she wanted to know how long she had left.

With a shambling gait, Sarah moved out of the shadow of the building, seeking a clear view in every direction, leaving a red-carpet trail in her wake. Already the red chilli sting of infection flowered and flowed. She might as well surf the red tide.

Shaky fingers made her fumble in her belongings, wasting precious seconds. The timepiece she at last took out was no clock and no plain chronometer. She spun dials and pressed buttons — the device set to her physicality. The object, detested, ever since the day Kevin handed the device over, whirred. His carefree sounding advice of "One day you might be grateful" now proved too prophetic, once more reminding her of old tales of one-eyed savage giants. Kevin's laughter haunted her — he'd called his contraption Cyclops. How could anyone blame them for their fierce natures if, as one fable stated, they noted the moment of their demise long before their time?

Clever bastard. The circumstances couldn't be any more dire, but still she smiled, something she'd not done in a long while. This was not his only creation. Her man... she'd always known he was more intelligent than most people suspected. Kind of liked it. Intelligence was sexy.

Her smile slipped. While she appreciated much of what he created, Cyclops was the least of his inventions to admire. She'd taken the gadget to please the love of her life, positive she'd never use it, unable to envision a time when they might be apart, one of them dying without the other. The mechanism buzzed, making her flinch when the tool pinged.

How long did she have?

One hour and ten. Four minutes of which were used, wasted.

First concern — to bind her wound. Doing so wouldn't provide her with a longer life expectancy, but if she didn't stop the blood flow, the unavoidable weakness might shorten the time remaining. Things required organising, completing before she died.

Priority: return to Kevin, say hello, say goodbye. The trip back required twenty minutes, plenty of time, but before she went, she had an errand to run.

To find Clyde. To kill him.

**** 

1:12 p.m.

Regret chewed into her intestines. What was wrong with her? She knew better than to trust him. Everything Clyde touched became a clusterfuck. Kevin would tell her not to be so hard on herself. Repeat the simple fact, it was easy to grow relaxed. Same as with the perambulating departed. A few quiet days and alertness faded.

Clyde, though… Hard to grow used to having him around. An ever present irritation she allowed to guard her back because she'd assumed he'd be slow on his feet and the zombies might jump him instead of her, which they had a few minutes before. She counted on him wailing like a baby and having to save him, not on his panic. More surprising was his strength and willingness to throw the starving corpse at her to save his own skin. She might not have much cared for him, but she would never have done that.

Calculated. The assessment was so clear in his eyes, despite his fright.

Their being used to this part of town being quiet was the thing, and when faced with the unexpected, he hadn't thought of the consequences. He reacted as he always did — put his survival before all else, before everyone. Same behaviour he displayed before the world went to hell, working alongside Kevin, in engineering. Apparently, the cretin understood nothing of the job they supposed him capable of, but his gab sure was gifted. When the other employees worked out what he was, well, by then it was hard to get rid of him.

Wasn't fair. So many floated through life unfairly, Clyde a prime example. There was often one in the workplace like that — pretending greater knowledge while knowing nothing. Excellent at hiding.

Well, he had better hide now because he'd killed her, and she sought vengeance.

A makeshift bandage in place, ragged raw aperture secure, only the pain endured. Without the discomfort, another minute passed in pretence of a future. The struggle to care brought tears to her eyes where the pain she suffered failed to. She and her husband continued because of a mutual promise. The whole human race might be doomed, and Clyde existed on equally borrowed time. He'd never survive alone, and he couldn't return to the little spot she had eked out with Kevin, not without her.

Sarah backtracked to the car and slid in behind the steering wheel. At which point, hysteria overcame her, humour as sharp as the alkaline sting of bile. She always hated to drive before now — too many cars on the road, driven by too many crazy, unskilled people. Took an apocalypse to make her handle a car again.

Damn. Her mind wandered. A waste of mental alacrity when she needed to hold things together. Fortunately, she'd taken the key from the car and Clyde didn't know how to hot-wire. He knew little about anything mechanical. Not to the level he should. He wouldn't have gone far on foot, and he'd be squealing at his shadow.

With luck, he feared her as much as he feared the zombies. He should.

Before she hunted, she needed sustenance. She was dying, but blood loss coupled with the infection proved debilitating. She spared another two minutes, dragged out what little was in the glove compartment and gobbled everything. What a joke — her last meal, one of stale crackers, melting chocolate biscuits, and a slug of warm water. Still, she savoured every bite, trying to appreciate the rich flavour of cocoa and sugar, this being her last blissful treat.

A glance at the time told her she had no more to squander, so she swallowed the last morsel in haste and fired the ignition. She trundled a short way down the road, letting the engine tick over, keeping the speed slow. No need to alert Clyde to her approach, and she didn't have far to go. Didn't require a detective to work out where the idiot tried to hide. As she got out of the car, the sun went behind a cloud. Didn't appear as though the day would brighten now, so another note of melancholy darkened the hour — she had enjoyed the last warm rays she would ever feel on her face.

****

1:17 p.m.

The house he owned was too far away for him to run to — even Clyde must realise his time was deficient in the number of minutes remaining. Easy to guess he'd hole up somewhere he presumed she wouldn't think to look — the place she might dismiss for being too obvious. Sarah didn't doubt his need for reassurance guiding his actions. The rat scampered to what he found familiar.

Parking at the top of the lane so as not to alarm her prey, she adopted a light jog, ears alert, gaze darting every which way as she pounded the ground beneath her feet. The road stayed quiet, but displayed signs of long ago struggles, splashes of intestinal ichor, and unidentifiable gore. Difficult to assess what emotion to latch onto — sorrow for those who fought and died here, or grateful the struggle happened long before.

She spotted the familiar silver van without a problem. The vehicle sat over to one side, doors open, appearing to rust … until she grew closer and recognised dried blood.

Drops of rain fell as she approached the red-brick wall of a building of two levels. Rain often hid the scent of the living from the dead, but also vice versa. Though falling water lessened smells, it also stifled all other sounds. Dry weather or wet, getting hold of Clyde, keeping him alive until she was ready to kill him would be awkward. She wanted him dead … but not yet.

The door stood ajar, made her stop to consider. Doubtless a trick. Clyde had slipped in and closed the door after him, but not tight, having chosen to make the place appear unoccupied, vulnerable to attack. Good thing the gap proved wide enough for her to ease into the interior without the need to push it further. No need to make a noise. Took much wriggling, but soon she stood in the gloom, straining her hearing. A threat might loom behind any of the hulking appliances that took up the shop floor.

8

Kevin and Clyde had worked here, and, though she didn't remember the exact layout, she recalled enough of the details. Snippets learned during Kevin's complaints concerning the lazy git of a colleague. She located Kevin's workspace and paused a moment to linger. There was no evidence of his ever being here, though she had no way to know what was out of place in this alien landscape, but she sensed the ghost of his presence.

Enough nostalgia. She was here for a reason and didn't expect to find Clyde at once or easily. Still, she checked the immediate areas. Kevin was right and someone might kill themselves in the stores because Clyde allowed them to be a sight to make eyes sore. Still, she peered among the debris, searched more for signs of the undead than an overweight man past middle age with ideas of grandeur.

Where would he be? Sarah dragged the depths of her memory. When the outbreak occurred, Clyde had followed Kevin home, wailing over what to do, having nowhere to go, his wife having absconded as cargo, floating away on his precious boat he was always going on about.

She bet a pile of food he wished he could sail away now.

****

1:23 p.m.

Apparatus similar to huge vending machines stood in rows. Magnolia walls, grey floors, grey mats. Without power and, therefore, fluorescent lighting, she mourned for extra windows, although there was more light here than she had expected.

Though the need to search was undeniable, she had grown to hate entering buildings more than she dreaded facing the dead on the street. She always longed for open spaces, and she and Kevin once promised each other it was what they would do — get away from the zoo called civilisation. They hadn't expected the end of the world, and she had now chosen an unconventional outcome, since she was turning into one of the undead and all, but what was a girl to do? Every person played the cards handed to them.

Her mind wandered to darker places, her longtime love of revenge stories. She hadn't expected to achieve an act of karma. A gun would be better than her knives, but … Sarah sighed, sparing the countdown on Cyclops a glance. Time ran away like the rain outside sluicing down the drains. Clyde must be upstairs. She hustled.

****

1:32 p.m.

He wasn't. Sarah circled, swearing under her breath. Precious moments misspent searching in a place she was certain he'd be, while risking a heart attack with every shift, susurration, or crack of sound. Rotten enough, but while she lingered upstairs, he might have gone past her, escaped, moved on to some place else. He might never have been here at all.

*Idiot!* One last curse and internal expletives mostly concerning her personal stupidity fell silent at the sight of a tall man, beer gut, red overall, as he rounded the corner and rushed her. Sarah opened her mouth to shout — names of people who had worked here flashing through her mind, a vague plan to tell the bloke she was no threat, but then she spied his snarl, an angry rictus of longing. No amount of talking was worth her while. He was fast, as if he'd died yesterday, so unlike the lumbering creatures often encountered. She was dead already, but the fear was natural, yet still she bit down on the scream bubbling up in her throat. No way to know whether another bite might alter the countdown, but time was the most important issue, and she wouldn't take a chance. Besides, another injury would still hurt, and might disable her.

No point trying to inflict damage on a zombie's genitals. Sarah went for metal — a stainless steel bar, if she wasn't mistaken. A grin split her face. Some information Kevin imparted had sunk in over the years. At the last second, Sarah stepped to the side, braced the bar, and impetus did the rest. The impaled bloated stomach of the zombie erupted, the foul stench a toxic mushroom. Holding her breath, she turned, pushed, continued his momentum. The metal speared deeper, and she carried through, cracking his skull into the machine's siding. Didn't stun him but broke a few teeth. *The less with which to eat me.*

The precious seconds gave her time to wind a strap through his belt. A pull on the chains hoisted him to his toes. To make sure, she threw another chain around the metal rod and wedged it. Shafted and stuck, the dead man couldn't turn and didn't have the brain capacity to pull free. Where the hell had he come from? More importantly, would his presence have kept Clyde away?

Not necessarily. He might have risked it or he and the zombie missed each other. Every chance existed that Clyde might be here, but where? Should she take the risk of using the time she had left to find him? Her throat closed; she groaned. Safe again for the moment but shaken, Sarah stumbled into the office, collapsed in a chair, swivelling to face the door.

Her chest was hollow as her heart died and shrivelled. Fatigue weighed in. The life she and Kevin had hoped to live existed a blink away. This was all a dream. Must be. Sarah lifted her head, swallowed. Time ticked on, and she didn't have any to spare, but imagination and despair gripped her. The vision of a world carrying on without her made her a ghost already. No way was she the first human to face her mortality or try to imagine a world empty of her presence. Kevin abiding in that empty house without her. What would become of him?

If humans became extinct, she struggled to define that as a terrible thing, but still struggled to confront her own death, when someone had taken her life away instead of her losing it. Grief crept into her consciousness. She sniffed, blinked away tears. Her hands came into focus. When had she lowered her head again? Now her chest ached. Better this all end, but not before she was finished.

"You're a useless fuck, d'you know, Clyde? Lying about what you could do. Earning too much, more than you deserved, laughing over the things you got away with at work. Bullying. Victimising. Throwing things on other people's desks because you didn't bother to do your job. Spending too much, pretending to live a lifestyle you couldn't afford. Showing no sympathy to sick or dying colleagues. D'you think Kevin didn't tell me? If you had a brain cell, you'd be dangerous."

Sarah rose, kicked the chair back and peered down, more surprised Clyde fitted under his desk than the fact he'd been stupid enough to curl up in the space beneath.

"Are you going to come quietly?"

Clyde's enormous round eyes stared up at her. He opened his mouth … perhaps to plead, perhaps to argue. What came out was a pained keening that called to her anger as well as her grief.

He chose not to cooperate, but she took him anyhow.

****

1:50 p.m.

One more check of the chronometer told her to hurry. She patted Clyde on the leg, closed the car's boot, by which time he was mewling.

****

2:06 p.m.

The drive deducted another twelve minutes — would have gone faster if not for the need to skirt around debris — but Clyde stole more of her minutes as she fought to pry him out of the car. She tried to be kind, but in the end, she stabbed him. Small jabs in places, warnings of pain, and the idiot responded to them, instead of fighting back. What did he think was happening here? When he tried to kick her, she stabbed him in the shins until he started crying and did as she asked. He walked into the house, shuffling like a zombie, hampered by the chains she'd looped around him. When she pulled them, he had to bend at the waist, and if he fell on his face, she planned to drag him. Believing her word, he hopped up the steps into the house without further threats.

He pleaded then, but she didn't listen, fastened him to the stove in the kitchen with the one heavy-duty padlock she had left. Not perfect — given an hour or two, he'd escape — but for the short time remaining, the fastening would do. No way could Clyde free himself in mere minutes, and then Kevin would take care of him. She moved all sharp implements out of his reach and went through to the living room.

Kevin turned his head to peer at her, blinking. Most days she swore he still recognised her, though whether by sight, scent, or something more primal, it was impossible to tell. Sometimes, she allowed him to touch her, one finger reaching out, stroking a line down her face.

He did so now as she knelt in front of him.

She apologised — silently, no words falling from her lips — for lacking the courage to lay him to rest, then to join him. It's what people did when someone beloved died, wasn't it? They continued because they just did.

Life and death … and love were funny things. If he didn't have this way of looking at her, as if he still knew her, it would be easier.

"I waited too long." She spoke aloud, tone asking him to forgive her. For waiting for him to show greater signs of decay to help her make peace with ending him, one day blending into the next until … here they were, facing the end together.

Perhaps it was better this way. The decision made for her.

"Hello, love, I'm home." Pointless chitchat. She smiled at him, reaching to undo his chains, no longer caring whether he attacked her. Not that he did. The infection must be too rife in her now for him to see her as any creature but another zombie. She burned, yet was dry inside. Shaking apart as her muscles cramped. The pain proved welcome as the only thing to keep her alert. "It's okay," she said. "This is enough for both of us. We'll be together."

No candlelight, but rain fell, and storm clouds moved nearer. The pinpricks of light which seeped through boarded windows faded. The setting bordered on romantic.

She opened the door, not bothering to lead. They'd find the path into the kitchen when ready for dinner.

****

2:15 p.m.

Well, what did she know? Kevin would be so proud. His chronometer device worked perfectly.

$Gaaarrrraaaghhhh.

## *The End*

# The Parting by Sandy DeLuca

He left her,
glancing back,
dark eyes smoldering,
a drop of crimson on his lips.

Footsteps sounded
on stairs,
whistling a somber tune.

Next, the roar of bikes—
men talking...

She peered from her window.

Below on the street—
dozens of them,
Harley's revving,
painted with bright colors,
spiraling designs, intricate,
painstakingly delineated;
stunning beneath the lifting horizon.
And the bike that Charlie mounted...
the most beautiful...
black thorny branches,
ravens flying above,
feathers black,
shades of purple and deep red.
And those bikers—white-faced (too white),
eyes dark,
bodies lean and tough,

And they drove away,
forming a single line,
past the shore.
its waves shimmering—
silvery...
as the dead
escaped the rising sun...

# La Citadel de Sangre*
## by
## Marge Simon

Bumming around Spain the summer after college, me and my buddy Garth stopped in the village of Tabernas. Both of us were keen to check out this one place in particular - the Citadel, at the edge of the desert. Lots of folklore about it.

When we got to Alamira, I asked an old woman about it. "La Ciudadela? *Si*. It's an ancient fortress, a sanctuary built by an ancient civilization to keep out demons. But beware, *a hijo mio,* it's no sanctuary now!" When I asked what she meant, she shook her head, muttering, "*Los que beben sangre!*"

Garth checked his Spanish pocket dictionary. "Way cool! She means 'those who drink blood.'" He looked up, grinning. "Like I'm scared, dude," he whispered to me. The guy running the tourist office talked us into taking along his daughter as a guide. Carmillita was a weird little gal with stringy dark curls, but she spoke good English. Something about her made me uncomfortable, but Garth thought she was hot.

Our shirts were soaked with sweat when we finally arrived at the Citadel. It was a sturdy structure, made from yellow native stone. We relaxed in the cool interior. I found a wine stash and we downed a couple bottles. Garth and the gal were enjoying some primo Spanish grass and talking. Last I noticed, she was licking his neck. Threesomes weren't my style. I nodded off after dusk.

"Wake up, buddy. Carmillita wants you with us." It was Garth's voice next to me in the dark. That gal was crouching beside him, eyes glowing red in the dark.

"Huh?" I asked sleepily.

"It ain't for sex, dude." A sudden flash of white fangs in the moonlight, his mouth on my neck. He stopped sucking to grin at me, blood streaming down his chin. "That gal sure knows how to party, man!"

### The End

*While researching this, I discovered this: https://eamon.wiki/The_Citadel_of_Blood, a longer story based on a citadel much like the one in this fiction. And a lot scarier.*

## Muse of the Maniac by Matthew Wilson

My muse has left me
Though I write on the wall
In the blood of my victims
With no whisper of a muse at all.

# In Black Boxes
## by
## Hillary Lyon

Jeremy pushed through the kitchen's swinging door, carrying a rectangular black cardboard box. He set it down on the bar and popped the plastic spigot. He then set about arranging the wine glasses next to the box.

"Please tell me you're not serious about serving *that* to our guests," Shelley whined. "They'll think we have no class—and we so want to be accepted by the residents of this neighborhood."

"They'll think it's a hoot." Jeremy grinned. "Besides, it's locally sourced; very small carbon footprint associated with its production." He tapped the box. "And remember, I had a sample taste at the store, where this precious juice is efficiently extracted."

As Shelley gave him a doubtful, tight-lipped smile, Jeremy added, "I found it to be quite delicious."

"But a beverage in a box! It's so, so—" Shelley searched her brain for a piercing pejorative; she failed. "Tacky."

"You worry way too much about what other people think," Jeremy said, turning to face his wife. He moved over to her and, intending to express reassurance, hugged her. "People—including our guests—*always* have an appetite for free stuff. They won't be terribly picky. Besides," he said, breaking his embrace and starting back toward the kitchen, "I bought six 3-liter boxes, so yeah, it's what we're serving."

****

The doorbell rang at exactly 9:00 p.m.

Jeremy tugged at the ruffled cuffs of his poet shirt. "Somebody's eager," he scoffed. He pressed a button on their music player, and the air filled with melancholy chamber music.

"They should know to be fashionably late." Shelley pouted. "I still have to light all the scented candles."

"Should've done that an *hour* ago," Jeremy chided. "That's what Martha advises." Bringing up Martha Stewart never failed to panic Shelley; it made her feel inadequate. Jeremy's cruel streak hungered to undermine Shelley's confidence; he fed it on a regular basis.

Jeremy strolled over to the front door and flung it open. It was Marley, the aged doctor who dwelled down the lane. Both men bowed deeply. With a grand sweep of his arm, Jeremy welcomed their first guest. "Come in, come in, my lovely, wicked friend!"

For the next hour, Jeremy repeated this performance until all their guests had arrived.

Marley was the first to partake of the ruby-esque fluid flowing from the black cardboard box. He held his full wine glass aloft, admiring how the light from the chandelier barely passed through the liquid. "Very nice!" he proclaimed before tasting the beverage. He took a tentative sip, then greedily slugged the remainder in his glass. Finished, Marley wiped the corners of his mouth with his lace-trimmed handkerchief. "Now that packs a wallop."

Everyone laughed, including Shelley. *It passed the connoisseur's taste test!* she noted with relief. *And if Marley approves—which he obviously does—all present will follow his lead.* Jeremy caught her eye and winked. Their guests gathered around the bar, politely nudging each other out of the way to get to the contents of the black box.

Jeremy leaned into Shelley to stage-whisper, "I'll bring out a few more boxes." Marley overheard this and nodded with approval.

The partygoers drained all six boxes by the time the evening's festivities concluded. Jeremy upended the last box, shaking the final few drops into Marley's glass. "Another dead soldier." Jeremy giggled, tossing aside the empty box.

Marley chortled at the idiom, then tipped the glass so that the drops slid down and dripped onto the tip of his wriggling forked tongue. He then licked the inside of his wine glass clean.

The room was silent. Marley scanned the den, nodding to each guest. At last, he cried, "All done!" Everyone clapped. *Our housewarming party was a success!* Shelley rejoiced to herself. She was so happy; she could have cried tears of blood.

"'Twas a delightful evening," Regina crowed as she grabbed her vintage cashmere shawl. "Especially those black boxes. How ingeniously efficient, how —"

"Modern," Byron added, pulling on his black leather duster.

"Urbane," Simone offered, sliding her silver mink stole over her cool, pale shoulders.

"Trendy," Mortimer sniffed, knotting the ties of his cloak. "It was savory, I will admit, but putting something so precious in a *box* —"

"Oh, shut up, Mortimer, or I'll put *you* back in a box," Regina snipped, to much laughter from the remaining partiers, "and bury you so deep underground no one will remember — or care — where you are."

****

"Save the cleanup for tomorrow," Jeremy murmured, hugging Shelley from behind. He kissed her neck, nibbling at the two scarred-over punctures above her jugular vein. "Remember when I —"

Shelley play-struggled, giggling like a schoolgirl engaging in her first awkward make out session. Her flesh would have erupted in goosebumps if she had still been warm-blooded. She loved this game.

"And remember when you came to my viewing? I was laid out in my Sunday best — thanks, Mom!" His ensuing laugh more resembled a low growl. "You hardly knew me, but you cried." Jeremy licked her neck. "That's when I knew you'd be mine."

Set to repeat, the music on their player began again. Notes from violins, violas, and cellos swelled and cried and moaned.

He spun her around and roughly took her face in his hands, an action that never failed to thrill her. Even in death. "Admit it," he said through clenched teeth as his canines slowly extended. "Just like me — delicious things *do* come in black boxes."

### *The End*

# The Vampire's Kiss by Alexis Child

Your coal black eyes burn like a furnace
A fire in my spirit
You are my demon in the night

A sacrifice for your kind
A cross forsaken
With nocturnal hair and pale skin
Scorching my throat
A lost soul borrowed
With sensual bloodlettings
And weapons sacred and blessed

We surrender now to the eternal beast
Shunned by the light
Drowning in demonic feast
Crouching over your lovely corpse
I taste your seeping blood and flesh
Such pain in a hollow heart
A stake driven deep in the chest

Hands plunged deep into your cold
Condemned soul
Dark angel of night
I am horrified, petrified
Stalked by an eternal night
Of dark desire

Covering me with shadow and sin
Forget this world, live for the night
He takes a bite
He lures me in with his charm
His brutal bloodlust grows
A sacrificial goat
Shadows untold

Leaving a tantalizing dark scar
With acute markings
An animal shunned by the light
Full of heartbreak
I hide the tears with his spirit in a jar
Appearances can be deceiving
Vampires pick the best disguises
And often we disbelieve
Distraught I cry beneath a tree
"He's not the guy for me"

To your gods sacrifice and pray
On this darkling night
Who's the hunter?
And who's the prey?

But I think I must be dead
I am reminded of the old times
Ashes dance across my lips

With the weeping angels of death
Wolves howl in agony
The world is under their tongue
The moon bows to a throne of stars
With whisperings and wails of pain
Silence falls again and again
Beware the kiss of the living dead

We hide in the shadows
And long for the light
For we are vampires
Forever imprisoned by night
Blood is my life
I was your prey
The moon is my sun
Night is my day

## Sonnet of Sirens and Dark Angels by Todd Hanks

I'd walk all through a burning Hell for you,
and let the embers scorch my flaming feet.
The demons there that need a soul to eat
I'd feed, although my heart is just for you.
Enraptured like I heard a siren's song,
your laughter charms me. I would gladly leap
in Styx, its rapids churning over me.
They'd curl and swirl and I would listen long.

Dark angels perched like eagles clutching crags
can also sing, although their song is black.
Upon an altar I'd let them attack,
and tear my body, rip my clothes to rags,
to only be allowed to hold you tight,
throughout the creeping hours that is night.

# An Unwrapping
## by
## Rod Marsden

It was an event that should never have taken place anywhere. An Egyptian cadaver was brought to a small but well-furnished cottage near the English Channel. It had travelled quite a distance from its original burial site in the Valley of the Kings. It was not completely mindful of this journey. It had been dead such a long time.

Legend has it an Egyptian can only make it to the land of his ancestors if he is laid to rest in Egypt. For some time, Khufu had been with his parents and their parents. His wife had been there, and in time, his children. Suddenly, someone whisked him away from his afterlife to a place of darkness. He was frightened. His path was no longer clear. The people he knew and loved gone, taken from him, or was it he taken from them? Centuries of not being alone gone, perhaps forever.

Frank and Emma Todd had invited the neighbors over for the unveiling. A mummy they had bought at great expense was to be unwrapped. It was 1890, a year of British discovery and wonder. The Todd couple had made their fortune in the manufacture of woolen garments and, in retirement, had chosen a place by the channel.

A storm was brewing on the afternoon of the unwrapping. Neither Frank nor Emma thought much of this occurrence. There had been storms before, and so one on this day merely added a sense of foreboding for some of their guests. They had hired Professor Drake from Oxford to do the unwrapping. He gave a talk before doing so, which pleased all. The crack of thunder overhead added something sinister to what he told them of how Egypt was the proper place for this corpse and not Kent, England. He went on to say he should protest the sacrilege he was about to perform, the scissors at the ready.

Khufu didn't feel a thing as the bandages of ages were removed from him. All he had at first was a sense of longing that had been his companion since leaving the valley. The air in the Kent cottage was wrong. It was too crisp with the scent of nearby coastal flowers.

The first layer of wrappings was gone; a discovery was made. There was a jade necklace containing a scarab beetle. Professor Drake grabbed it and it was then the cadaver's hollow eye slits lit up green and a hand clamped down on the professor's wrist. Those in the room, including the professor, cried out. A pleasant afternoon's distraction had turned into something else.

Professor Drake freed himself from Khufu's grip by letting go of the necklace. There was a general sigh of relief. Frank bade the professor to go no further in the unwrapping but to replace what they had already taken from the ancient body. The professor did as he was instructed. The storm overhead ceased.

The very next day, they sent the mummy back to Egypt and to the Valley of the Kings with instructions to put it back where it was found. This didn't make sense to those who had taken it out in the first place, but the money was good and so they complied. Even so, they had to wonder why the long journey to England and then the equally long trip back. Was there something about this cadaver that pricked the consciousness of the English?

Once back where his corpse belonged, Khufu's spirit was once more in the land of his afterlife, where the flowers belonged along the Nile rather than the English Channel. He couldn't account for where he had been or why. He knew his talisman had intervened and had helped to bring him home.

*The End*


## Fear Itself by Marc Shapiro

For your consideration
Fear
Of The Dark
The demons
Unspeakable monsters
That rend
Tear
And bleed us
Fear is the noun
The verb
The adjective
Fear is with us 24/7
It makes middle of the night calls
When we are at our best
And our worst
Fear
When we are on top of the world
But can't imagine getting much higher
Fear
When we can't imagine getting much lower
Fear shows up to help
Think we could
Fear
It screams your name in the middle of the night
And let's you know
That it's not going anywhere

## Help Wanted by Marc Shapiro

Am I qualified
Let me see
Neck neck neck
Bite bite bite
Suck suck suck
Blood blood blood
Will only work nights
Do I get the job

23

# The Vigil
## by
## Lee Clark Zumpe

The night receded in degrees, leaving only familiar old shadows clawing at the alcoves. Bryant found himself in her bedroom, lingering alongside soft-muttered prayers and evaporated tears. For the first time that evening, Susan was alone. Bryant heard faint voices echo through the halls of the estate, heard her sisters gently sobbing downstairs.

Her brothers would not welcome him. In their eyes, he was to the family as much an affliction as the pestilence consuming poor Susan.

Boldly, Bryant stepped from the shadows.

Susan's eyelids fluttered. Bryant caressed her damp forehead. Beneath his icy touch, she burned with fever.

His own misfortune had kept him from seeing his daughter enter the world. He would not leave her side now.

When death arrived at dawn, she saw the young man perched nervously on her bedside. She stretched a trembling hand to touch him—but in that instant, he was gone.

### The End


## Imram by Lee Clark Zumpe

To an island set upon four pillars
Where time passes unnoticed.
No grieving, no winter, no want;
And home falls beneath the sediment
Of centuries.

To an island of the Otherworld
Where birds in harmony call.
No grave, no famine, no fear;
Yet home calls the wistful traveler
To return.

## Melpomene by Lee Clark Zumpe

Wearing the willow
Gnashing teeth
in this melting mood

Melpomene
dropping sighs
tragic mask in hand

Shedding sorrows
seducing the ready pen
language born of tear-laden ink.

# SPU
## by
## Ann Stolinsky

"Bubbie, let's play a game."

"Okay, Ava, what would you like to play?"

"The vocabulary game. I'll tell you a vocabulary and you have to tell me a food it's in and how to make that food."

"Don't you mean the ingredient game?"

"No," she pouted, yawned, and insisted, "the vocabulary game."

I looked at her via the rearview mirror. Her pouts are adorable. And I learned long ago not to argue with a tired, cranky child.

"Okay. Which vocabulary?"

"Cheese. You have to say a recipe with cheese in it. You start. Ask me."

"Okay. How do you make mac 'n cheese?"

"My favorite! The best part is the Velveeta!"

I turned my head over my right shoulder and smiled at my granddaughter in her car seat.

That's when my car ran over something in the road.

"Bubbie, it's raining!"

It is, but not raindrops. Thick red liquid oozed down my windshield.

"Ava, we're going to be delayed getting home. Why don't you take a nap? We can finish playing later."

"Okay, Bubbie."

The Weather Girls' song, "It's Raining Men," came to mind. Because it was raining body parts. A loud thud on my roof made me jump when something heavy landed on it. The metal buckled inward, thankfully not enough to hit either of us. I stopped the car, as did all the others on the road. I called 911.

Then I called my daughter, Sue.

"Sue, what's going on?"

"I've been called into work. Where are you, Mom?"

"On Route 1. Ava is asleep in the car."

"I'll be right there."

Two minutes later, I heard the familiar swoosh of my daughter's approach. She carried her husband in her arms. He waved to me as she gently lowered him to stand next to my car.

"Sorry, Mom, Drew was walking to work. I picked him up first."

"Not a problem."

Drew opened my car door quietly, and got in back with Ava, being careful not to wake his daughter.

"All buckled in?" Sue asked.

"Yes," Drew and I whispered in unison.

My daughter lifted my car above the others and flew it to our house.

Sometimes it's nice to have a superpowered child.

She put the car in the driveway in front of our house. Drew grabbed Ava, who had miraculously stayed asleep, and we ran inside. Sue quickly kissed us all, then flew off.

I looked at Drew and whispered, "You'd better shower and change before Ava realizes you've got blood on you."

I turned on the TV.

And heard a loud siren - the alert signal.

"Everyone, stay inside. Repeat, stay inside, unless you are a medical professional. Doctors, nurses, EMTs, you are needed immediately. Activate your alert signal, and someone will come to get you. Repeat, all citizens stay inside! Supers, report for duty to Super People United HQ! We need you!"

**** 

Several hours later, Sue breezed inside with her partner. My Sue, the Cyclone, and her partner, Matt, the Tremblor, looked exhausted.

I handed them both half-gallon jugs of water. They need to keep hydrated when they're working. They downed the water in minutes.

"Ava?" Sue asked after she finished her jug.

"Playing in her room."

"SPU HQ discovered the first body part a minute before you called me. The sky seemed to split open, and parts fell from the opening. The split moved, closing in one spot and opening in another: I've never seen anything like it. Apparently, this happened everywhere throughout the world."

Sue rubbed her forehead.

"I have a migraine. It's mind-boggling to imagine the number of body parts that came through from who knows where, that landed everywhere in the split's path. SPU partnered with the International Super People, INC, to try to stop the parts from falling and killing people."

Tremblor took up the story.

"We had to figure out what to do with the millions of arms, legs, whatever, that suddenly appeared. Scientists presume they came from another world, similar to ours, since the parts looked human. We piled all that we could find into refrigerated shipping containers, which Icy Girl froze, and they're in the Atlantic Ocean now. If anything can unite our world, this is it. Every scientist is salivating to get a shot at examining these pieces.

"Me, I'm exhausted, don't ever again want to see what I saw today. I'm going home, going to sleep for three days. Don't wake me."

**** 

Sue was normal until she turned eighteen. That year, many others her age also received powers. Scientists have no clue, a decade later, what happened to them. They've tested and retested the supers with no success in finding the origin of their powers. One percent of the world's population is super. Fewer teens exhibit new superpowers each year, but it hasn't stopped completely.

In this country, the government formed gated communities of homes for supers, several located in each state. Everyone who isn't super takes care of everyone else in the community. So far, this has helped to keep the families of the supers safe.

****

Body parts raining down stopped the next day, thankfully. The scientists have examined and re-examined and re-re-examined thousands of them. The DNA is just like ours. These are not our cousins; they are our brothers and sisters. And mothers and fathers. Scientists put samples in Petri dishes to see if any bacteria grow, thinking it could be biological warfare. They're frantically trying to determine where this phenomenon originated.

The scientists and military are also fighting over the rights to the body parts.

****

Two days later, letters fell from the sky. Letters the scientists presumed were from the people who died trying to get to us. Would they be letters telling us not to fight amongst ourselves? Warnings about climate change? Or warnings that they'll figure out how to come through whole and kill us all?

This is what the letters said:

"We sent through body parts from our prisoners. Our world is overcrowded. We needed to cull the population. We have been watching your world deteriorate for years. We figured we'd solve two problems at once, our overpopulation and your economy. We heard everything there costs an arm and a leg.

"You're welcome."

****

*Badda bing badda boom.* ☺

## Baptised by New Gods by Matthew Wilson

I don't like the old church
The ring of the bell
The drone of the priest
The burn of the holy water.

My family's bones are in its crypt
Things of night that met the day
And now its occupants sing
Their victory over the boiling of my blood.

I have prayers too
But my dead queen has left me
If she returned my powers
I would command lightning to destroy that place.

So now I hate the old church
Where I was baptised as human and then worse
And now a choir sings to their lord
Who closed the gates of heaven to my kind.

# Hunger Pangs
## by
## Hal Kempka

Martin stood in the kitchen, listening intently to the realtor's disclosure after reading Martin's purchase offer:

"Full disclosure requires me to inform you of any problems or known history of the residence. I have rented and sold this house several times, and no owner or tenant has stayed for more than a week. I've heard every excuse, from hearing weird sounds shortly after they settled in to complaints of a nauseating stench that appeared when they tried to clean the walls or floor. Most have just disappeared, vacating the house in the middle of the night and leaving their belongings behind. Most of what they all left is still piled up in the basement. In short, they all breached their contracts by implying it was haunted."

The realtor sounded a little sheepish and appeared to be waiting for Martin's response with the expectation he would rescind his offer and request to see another property. So many before him had. Martin, however, just shrugged and glanced around the room.

The checkered tile floor appeared cracked and worn, though its color had not seemed to fade much. The torn and sun-faded window drapes adorning the filmy dirty windows would go, and the fifties style stove, refrigerator, and scarred and paint-flaked table and chairs would have to be replaced.

"Frankly," he replied, "I plan to remodel the place. The floors and wood frame appear sturdy and in good shape, but it's an old house that will require a lot of work. I'm certain the prior owners realized they were in well over their heads and couldn't afford the upgrade and upkeep costs required to return it to its previous splendor."

The realtor raised his eyebrows, and his cheeks bulged with an exhale of relief. "Well, in that case, let's take care of the paperwork, shall we?"

Martin struggled to hide a smug smile while the realtor bent to retrieve the paperwork from his briefcase. He deliberately made an offer far lower than the realtor's listing price. It had been on and off the market numerous times, and he felt sure his realtor wanted an opportunity to wash his hands of the albatross.

On move-in day, Martin stood outside the house waiting for the moving van. He gazed up at the aging Victorian, admiring the stately but cracked and discolored brick structure, wraparound porch and pillars, and the ornate but paint-flaked window sills. He especially liked the cone-shaped roof on the corner and window-lined tower, as that was where he planned to put his office. Once he corrected the varying states of disrepair and returned the aging house to the glory of its heyday, he'd stay a few years and then sell it for a massive profit.

He spent the next week going room to room, noting the repairs and remodeling that would be needed. After settling in and sorting out the furniture and knickknacks to be discarded on the upper floors, he decided to take advantage of the warm summer day and tackle sorting and cleaning the basement.

The wooden basement stairs hugged the damp brick wall, and as Martin descended, the pungent odor of dust and age that hung in every room of the long-neglected house now turned damp and sharp with the heavy stench of mildew. He shivered as a slight chill swept through him.

The wooden stairs creaked with every step, and slivers protruded from the cracked and aging wood. Upon reaching the basement floor, he crossed the room to open the cellar windows for fresh air. Martin's nostrils flared as he breathed in the welcome aroma of the lilacs planted alongside the house. The scent soothed his stinging nostrils.

Years of boxes and discarded furniture left by prior occupants littered the basement floor. He sorted through the dusty items and stacked the ones he wanted against the wall beneath the windows. The unusable items he didn't think he could sell online or to an antique store were relegated to the trash bin in the alley.

Martin's sweat-drenched shirt clung to his back, and the slivers of sunlight shafting through the windows revealed the sparkling, iridescent glow of what he perceived as mildew on his dusty shoes.

A faucet that apparently once emptied into a now-gone wash basin protruded through one wall. He rolled up his pant legs, removed his shoes and socks, and turned the spigot. He wiggled his toes, enjoying the cool spray that felt good on his sweaty feet.

Water welled up around the floor drain and funneled through an apparent semi-clogged pipe, emitting a deep guttural sound that resembled an old man gargling. Martin chuckled to himself, thinking that was the closest sound he'd heard since moving in that a prior tenant might have mistaken for evidence of haunting. The other sounds appeared to be nothing more than the aches and pains that an aging house would exhibit.

He left his shoes by the stairs and continued to sort through boxes. At sundown, the light dissipated and the basemen shadows lengthened. He decided to quit for the day and rinsed his feet. As he did so, Martin noticed how his feet sparkled from the mildewy floor.

That evening Martin poured a glass of wine and settled onto the couch to watch television. After a while, he noticed he'd been absentmindedly rubbing the arch of one foot with the other. He scratched until the itch stopped.

It began again a little later, and Martin scraped the bottom of his foot back and forth against the carpet until the itch finally went away. He retired for the evening and awakened a few hours later, his feet itching again. He again scratched them, then tossed and turned until he finally fell asleep.

The next morning, he picked up a bottle of calamine lotion from the drugstore before cleaning more of the cellar. That evening before retiring, he slathered the ointment on his feet and legs. The lotion felt cool on his skin, and he soon fell asleep, exhausted.

When the itch began again, he awakened and glanced at the clock on the nightstand. One in the morning.

"Shit!" he grumbled, and scratched his itching feet. The itch slowly moved up his calves and over his knees. The more he scratched, the higher it moved. When it reached his testicles, he doubled over from a sharp stabbing pain that felt like he'd been kicked in the balls. Thankfully, it lasted but a few seconds.

Martin jumped from the bed and hurried into the bathroom. The light stabbed at his eyes as he flipped the wall switch. He sat back on the toilet seat and examined himself.

His testicles were swollen and the heavy scratching had irritated the skin even more. After coating his crotch and scrotum with more calamine lotion, he emitted a deep sigh while it soothed his raw and reddened skin.

The itch finally went away, and Martin returned to bed. He fell onto it, exhausted, and the next he knew, the sun shining through the window woke him. He hurried to the bathroom and turned on the shower. He stood beneath the cool shower, letting the water flow over his shoulders and body.

When the itch began once again, Martin grumbled. "No, not again," and feverishly scratched and rubbed at his entire body.

As the itch moved up to his ribs, something beneath his skin moved from one side to the other, as though evading his scraping fingers. He panicked when the itching rose past his neck; It stopped at the ear canal and again increased in intensity.

The more Martin scratched at the ear canal, the more the itch moved deeper into his ear. He jammed his finger hard, unable to stop it. When his eardrums burst, his screams of pain sounded like a far-off echo.

He'd lost all sense of self, and his nails tore at the skin and muscle. His fingernail ruptured the cochlea and broke apart the tiny bones of his middle ear. His head felt like it would explode, and he passed out from the excruciating pain, unable to hear his horrific screams.

Several minutes later, Martin's corpse began to undulate. It inched toward the door, leaving an odorous and sticky, sparkling trail in its wake. The liquifying body slithered across the floor, down the hall to the stairs, and through the house to the basement.

The stairs soaked up the moving corpse's slime, and his body's decomposition began to show. It undulated to the middle of the basement floor, and wormlike strings of slime oozed from Martin's body. They slithered into the walls, nourishing them.

In the dark quiet of the old Victorian, the walls and floor emitted a low moan, their hunger pangs sated for now. Repeated creaks in the walls emanated through the house while it settled back to await another buyer. This owner had only been a snack, and they needed to have a family that would provide them with a real, homemade meal.

## *The End*

## Changing Perspectives by Marge Simon

She recalls the days before she was turned,
late summer days with scents of lilac and rose.
She'd twist them in her hair, wear them tucked in buttonholes.
Those long afternoons when she would spend hours
sipping Zinfandel from a crystal glass,
trying different shades of lipstick while
admiring her mirrored image; it was a time of
of guileless indulgence, but that was before.

She still has sweet summer evenings,
though the blossoms have died on the vine;
mirrors no longer return her reflection, but
blood is a far sweeter drink than wine.

# The Last Confession
## by
## Linda Barrett

The gaunt woman wrapped in her concealing black cloak hurried into St. Stephen's Anglican Church. Lowering the cloak's hood, she looked around her. She had dressed head to toe in black to keep out the sun's dangerous rays. Her nostrils took in the intense odor of incense. Memories flooded her mind of long-lost days when she walked the earth in various incarnations. She fought to keep the bloody tears from falling. Her immortal and immoral heart ached with the ancient sorrow of regret.

*How long have I run from God?* She wondered to herself.

"Can I help you?" a male voice asked her.

From behind her thick, dark sunglasses, her ebony eyes stared at the church's Gothic architecture. She thought of the memory of Paris during the Black Death before realizing she stood in the middle of the twenty-first century in Northampton, Pennsylvania. How long had she refused God's love and forgiveness?

"I said, how can I help you?" the male voice asked her again.

Disturbed from her musing, the silver-haired woman turned to face the young man in his black clerical suit.

"I want you to hear my confession," she said.

"You can confess to God. You need not go to me," the handsome young cleric said.

"Oh," the woman sighed. "A Protestant." She turned to leave.

"Wait!" the minister called. "If you want me to pray with you, I can."

The woman removed her hood and stared at him with her hollow, black eyes. The cleric gasped and recoiled a foot out of terror.

"Wait!" she shouted, her cry echoing in the church's high arched ceiling.

The holy man stepped over the altar's railing.

"We can pray over here," he said, gesturing with a shaking hand toward the pews.

They sat in adjoining pews, looking at each other. The minister's kind, brown eyes revealed he was a young man. She remembered Martin Luther was also a young man when she met him. He also reminded her of another young man, a shepherd in the hills who became a king.

"My name is Isabeau of Galtrey," the vampire began.

"Good to meet you. My name's Pete Newhouse."

They shook hands. Isabeau forgot to tell him something about them.

Reverend Pete wore a shocked expression as she gripped his hand. Her very touch caused him to cry out in pain. Isabeau drew back and shuddered.

"I'm sorry," she said. "I didn't know my hands were that cold."

Reverend Peter rubbed his hands between his legs.

"Cold hands." His teeth chattered as he tried to smile. "Warm heart."

Isabeau lowered her head.

"My heart was never warm. I have been one with the walking dead since the fall of Babylon." She sighed.

Reverend Peter twisted his brows together.

"Fall of Babylon?"

Isabeau nodded.

"I was a high priestess of Ishtar. The fertility goddess. I used to be very beautiful. I had many lovers during my station in life. Making love to me was like being in union with the goddess. It all started when I noticed the fine lines on my face growing deeper and deeper."

"It's a sad fact of life," Reverend Pete said. "We all grow old."

Isabeau wiped her tears with her sleeve.

"If I grew any older, I would be buried alive as a sacrifice," she cried in a strangled voice. "I couldn't risk that. So, I went to a sorcerer who gave me a potion. Little did I realize what would happen to me."

Reverend Pete rose and went to pick up a box of tissues from one of the sanctuary's windowsills. He handed it to her. She nodded a thank you as the tears dropped from her eyes.

Loudly blowing her nose, she continued with her story.

"I had to fight this urge to drink blood. I couldn't stand the daylight. I grew hard and bitter because I couldn't grow old. This hunger that controlled me enslaved me. I started out sacrificing animals. Then I graduated to killing innocent humans! The hunger compelled me to want more and more."

Isabeau doubled over, sobbing.

Reverend Pete reached out and stroked her head.

"Have you considered psychiatric counseling? Your delusions are frightening."

"They aren't delusions. I've been killing people for over 2,000 years. I've murdered my many lovers with this compulsion. I dabbled in the occult and beseeched so many gods and goddesses to save me. None have helped me. I performed rituals with the Aztecs, posing as one of their priests. I slaughtered all these innocent children and maidens. I traveled all over the globe to places to quench my hunger. After I left Babylon, I wandered into Israel and practiced my trade. I went into Roman temples and killed animals to satisfy my desires. Then, one day, I met a man."

"Where did you meet him?"

"In Israel," Isabeau snarled as she raised her head to him.

Reverend Pete's mouth dropped open, and his eyes widened. Isabeau realized she had shown him her fangs. Her shoulders slumped.

"I braved the daytime to come here to see you," she murmured as she stared off into space.

"What about the man?" Reverend Pete's voice broke the tense silence.

"He was a man who performed many miracles. He even rose from the dead."

"Yes," Reverend Pete said. "He's the reason why I'm here and not on Wall Street."

"I hated him!" Isabeau screamed in a combination of anger and regret. "I called myself a sorceress and performed many tricks, but he made me look foolish. His magic was far better than mine. He found me doing my magic. He came through the crowd with his companions. When our eyes met, he seemed to look right through me!" Isabeau screamed again, her voice bouncing off the sanctuary's walls.

"What did you do next?" Reverend Pete rose to his feet.

"I fled through the crowd. I couldn't go through all those bodies. There were so many of them. I turned around and faced him. We were eye to eye. He knew my every thought, even before it formed in my head." Isabeau gasped for air.

"He knew what was in a man." Reverend Pete sat down again.

"I knew he was God and I hated him. I wanted to beat him at his own game. He threatened my very existence as a sorceress. I'd never been so scared in my life. He reached out his hand and called me in my Babylonian name…."

"What was it like to come face to face with Our Lord?"

Isabeau stared down at her feet.

"He said, 'Repent and believe.' I had no way to fight him. He said, 'Your time of running is over. Face me and believe that I came to save even you.'"

"What did you do then?"

"I gathered my courage, changed into a black bird, and flew away. I flew as far as I could go."

"Where did you go?" Reverend Pete asked.

Isabeau buried her head in her hands. More bloody tears dropped from between her fingers.

"I landed in Rome and stayed there for many years. Then, I went to Iberia. That's Spain. I met a man there named Paul. He preached the same thing as did the one you call Jesus. I heard him and ran away from him again. How could he know about me? I continued in my evil ways until the centuries passed. I taught magic in the Byzantine Empire. Even when I had a coven of witches, the young rabbi's words still haunted me."

"So, you came to see me?" Reverend Pete said.

"I fought against Martin Luther and John Calvin. I faced witch hunters and priests. Even when I wasn't running, fear followed me. Even if I lived, I still couldn't remove my mind from him. All the sins I committed could not take away my shame. The Puritans in New England chased me. My life changed after I consulted Adolph Hitler with my astrology. After that, I wanted to change. But I couldn't get the chance."

"Until now." Reverend Pete nodded.

"What can I do?"

"Ask God to forgive you and ask Christ to save you."

Isabeau buried her face in her bony hands. Bloody tears ran down her fingers.

"Christ, help me! I come to you! Please don't cast me out."

A powerful beam of light streamed down from the window and covered Isabeau's dark-clad form. Isabeau's body became like powder. The dust that was her body floated through the beam, transforming into a white dove. The blindingly white fowl soared through the air and flew through the church's open door. Reverend Pete jumped to his feet and his mouth dropped open. What was left of the vampire collapsed to the floor.

Reverend Pete looked up and managed to speak.

"God is that merciful! This will make a great sermon." He smiled.

### *The End*

# The Bite of Love by Todd Hanks

Her eyes sparkled like
brown waves on lake
water when the sun comes
out after rain. But her
bite felt right just at
midnight when she
drank the blood rushing
like a subway train through
my trembling vein.

I had always felt as
disconnected as an
unplugged appliance.
But then I felt like a
part of her heart, and
one of the ancients.

She whispered to me
I had eternal life, as
we danced by the lake
on the sand, where the fire
on the shore burned
higher than before with
orange flames rising like
claws on the devil's hands.

# The Hunter's Mistake by Denny E. Marshall

Thousands of bats sleep
Hanging on cave ceiling
Vampire feels safe

Vampire hunter
Follows trail to giant cave
Thousands of choices

Using dynamite
Seal entrance permanently
Rides back into town

The harvest season
Insects eat all the crops
Farmers lynch the hunter

Many starve to death
Many more pack up and leave
Dust sweeps a ghost town

Wagon train heads west
In search of fertile pastures
A place to live

# Night Gallery

## Primordia: In Search of The Lost World

### Review by the Late Tom Johnson

- ➢ Title: Primordia: In Search of The Lost World
- ➢ Author: Greig Beck
- ➢ Genre: Science Fiction
- ➢ Publisher: Severed Press
- ➢ ISBN: 978-1925711479
- ➢ Price: $12.78 (Paperback); $4.99 (Kindle); 246 pages
- ➢ Available at: Amazon, Barnes & Noble, eBay, and other retailers
- ➢ Rating: 4 Stars

Ben Cartwright is out of the Army now and back home, but still looking for some excitement. Discovering that his namesake, Benjamin Cartwright, in 1908, had gone in search of the lost world, sending his notes and maps to Sir Arthur Conan Doyle in England. Doyle had written the fiction novel from those notes, and the actual lost world just might be real. Discussing it with his old friends, they decide to look for the fabled lost world themselves. However, they need the notes and maps entrusted to Sir Arthur Conan Doyle. The first hundred pages or so reminded me of the Hardy Boys solving puzzles as they search for the hidden notes and maps; another group is also after them, and the maps end up in the wrong hands. But that's okay; Ben's team has the notes, and the last hundred pages take them to the plateau. Here's where things get scary. A comet called Primordia passes close to Earth's orbit every ten years, and during its passing, one plateau becomes a time portal, returning the mountaintop millions of years in the past. It's this plateau they have found and climbed a chimney to the top, where they discover dinosaurs and giant snakes. It doesn't take long for everyone to be eaten except for Ben Cartwright and his girlfriend, Emma Wilson. Just as a giant 70-foot snake is about to eat them, Emma falls over the edge of a cliff and escapes into a cave. Ben is running from the monster snake when the comet leaves Earth's orbit once again. Emma makes it to civilization and vows to return to the plateau in ten years to save Ben.

The yarn was fun, and being based on Sir Arthur Conan Doyle's *The Lost World* made it unique. There weren't many dinosaurs, but we do see a few. Mostly, giant snakes eat everyone since they are the major predator on the mountaintop. Personally, I don't like reading a book that doesn't end, as this one is left open for part two. I would love to know what happens in the sequel, but a little afraid it will begin like Nancy Drew before we get to the meat of the book. After all, Emma must wait another ten years when the comet makes its next pass by Earth to attempt a rescue. Will Ben survive that long? And is it just a coincidence that the comet is named Primordia? Highly recommended.

Tom Johnson, Author of *Jur: A Story of Pre-Dawn Earth*

# Post Facto

## Review by the late Tom Johnson

- ➢ Title: Post Facto
- ➢ Author: Darryl Wimberley
- ➢ Genre: Mystery
- ➢ Publisher: The Permanent Press www.thepermanentpress.com
- ➢ ISBN: 978-1579625559
- ➢ Price: $19.46 (Hardback); $9.99 (Kindle); 248 pages
- ➢ Available at: Amazon, Barnes & Noble, OverDrive, and other retailers
- ➢ Rating: 4 Stars

Clara Sue Buchanan, a big city reporter, has returned to her home in Florida. She takes over the local newspaper and a local mystery. The Lambs, a local family, is trying to cheat Butch out of his inheritance. Butch is a little slow-witted and might lose everything without help. Clara teams with her cousin, the local sheriff, to investigate strange cases that seem supernatural. What's going on, and could she end up the next victim?

The publisher sent me a copy of the book for an honest review. This was a fun story and a slight play on the big city cop retiring to Florida to become involved in a murder case. But this time, it's a journalist and she's female. But everything else is in place. It is a neat plot and has good characterization, so it is already ahead of those retired cops moving to Florida plots, and well worth the read. Highly recommended.

Tom Johnson, Author of *Invitation to Murder*

# Tripl3 Cross

## Review by the late Tom Johnson

- ➢ Title: Tripl3 Cross
- ➢ Author: John Hegenberger
- ➢ Genre: Intrigue
- ➢ Publisher: Rough Edges Press
- ➢ ASIN: BOIIDOVI2C
- ➢ Price: $2.99 Kindle; 142 pages
- ➢ Available at: Amazon, Barnes & Noble, eBay, and other retailers
- ➢ Rating: 4 Stars

His dying mother tells Elliot Cross, a hard case private detective from Columbus, Ohio, that his missing father was still alive and needed his help. This is enough to start him on the cold trail, but when a CIA operative named Fred Lewis says he knows where the missing man is and that he was hiding from the mob, Elliot wants to learn more. Things start moving when he's introduced to another CIA operative named Ellen Nuevitas. He is taken to CIA Headquarters to view records but finds they've been moved. Later he finds Fred Lewis dying from a bullet wound and is told in a dying breath that his father is in Cuba. This begins the trail to reach Cuba in search of his father, where he finds lies and hidden motives from everyone involved.

The story is well-written, and the plot complicated. With all the twists, no one may be who they are supposed to be, and some stuff seems to come from left field, at times muddying the water. I also found it a little curious the way Elliot is allowed to run around with a high government official with no questions asked by his superiors, and regardless of the widespread corruption, there are always checks and balances, even within Cuban politics. But the author gives us a dandy yarn to pass a few hours in a good book.

Tom Johnson, Author of *Detective Mystery Stories*

# A Dollar Short and a Day Late

## Review by the late Tom Johnson

- ➢ Title: A Dollar Short and a Day Late
- ➢ Author: R. Archer
- ➢ Genre: Tongue-in-cheek Noir
- ➢ ASIN: B00ZK8XYHS
- ➢ Price: $1.49; 10 pages
- ➢ Available on Amazon Kindle
- ➢ Rating: 5 Stars

*"Lighthearted Tongue-in-cheek."*

Johnny Dollar, a freelance insurance investigator, is so busy he needs a secretary to take care of the bookwork, filing, and answering the phone. He can't believe his good luck when sexy Rita Longmire shows up to interview for the job, claiming to know all about a secretary's duties. But within only a few days, it appears that beauty may be all the talent she has.

This was a fun read. Though Johnny doesn't have a case to investigate, he does learn that finding a good secretary may not be as easy as he imagined. Growing up listening to radio drama, *Yours Truly, Johnny Dollar,* was one of the best dramas on the air. It's great to see him back, and we look forward to his next case from the author. Short stories have almost disappeared from mainstream literature, and we no longer have the many genre magazines available for short story format at the local newsstand. The author is bringing them back with a bang, and we love it. I read this one while drinking my first cup of coffee. Highly recommended.

Tom Johnson, Author of *Detective Mystery Stories*

# Al Clark (Book One)

## Review by the late Tom Johnson

- ➢ Title: Al Clark (Book One)

- Author: Jonathan G. Meyer
- Genre: Science Fiction
- Independent Publishing Platform
- ISBN: 978-1720011910
- Price: $11.95 (Paperback); $3.99 (Kindle); 286 pages
- Available at: Amazon, Barnes & Noble, Google, and other retailers
- Rating: 5 Stars

*"Character Driven Science Fiction"*

Waking up on a spaceship orbiting a planet, a man remembers nothing of his past. A faded placard appears to read "Al Clark," so that's all he has to go by. Roaming the giant ship, he finds a young boy named Chris, who has only been awake for a while. Eventually, they discover other bodies in stasis and begin reviving them. Out of 1000 passengers, only a little over 800 have survived. Below the ship is the planet Avalon, their destination. They arrived ten years previous, so something went wrong and the awakening never happened on schedule. Now the process begins of moving the survivors to Avalon and starting their human race over. It looks like a peaceful planet, and they meet another race of human-like friendly people. But their valley isn't peaceful. Dinosaurs still rule this planet, and they will have to prove mightier or be destroyed.

The story is character-driven, and the reader feels for them and follows their conquest of the terror and the discovery of who they really are. The author knows how to pull the reader into the story. A great story that could have appeared in the classic science fiction period of the 1950s. Highly recommended.

Tom Johnson, Author of *Worlds of Tomorrow*

# Fangs and Claws

## Review by the late Tom Johnson

- Title: Fangs and Claws
- Author: Cameron Joseph
- Genre: Horror
- Publisher: Independent Publishing Platform
- ASIN: B076YNXH9G
- Price $0.00; 63 pages
- Available at: Amazon, Barnes & Noble, Walmart, and other retailers
- Rating: 4 Stars

Ballard Stone buys a large area of land with a tract of forest with trees that reach the heavens. He sends his nephews, Seath and Duncan, to the forest as workers. He has already sent in his crew boss and foreman. The boys take their girlfriends along for the adventure, but there is already someone else in the woods: Raven Shadow, a witch, and her companion, a huge half-man, half-beast, over seven foot tall, with a sabertooth cat head, and fierce claws. Raven is determined that Ballard Stone will not have his way.

A fun read, but perhaps would have been better read around a creepy campfire on a dark night. The book, even short, would have benefited from an editor or at least a proof-reader. It reminded me of some slasher/sex teenager movies from the 1970s and '80s. The language, slashing, and sex could have been cleaned up to give us a great yarn with witches and monsters. Highly recommended.

Tom Johnson, Author of *Carnival of Death*

# Jericho's Trumpet

## Review by the late Tom Johnson

- ➢ Title: Jericho's Trumpet
- ➢ Author: Robert Gallant
- ➢ Genre: Action Thriller
- ➢ Publisher: Independent Publishing Platform
- ➢ ISBN: 978-0578208107
- ➢ Price: $11.99 (Paperback); Free (Kindle); 287 pages
- ➢ Available at: Amazon, Thrift Books, Google, and other retailers
- ➢ Rating: 4 Stars

Travis Weld works for a secret government group that searches for and kills terrorist groups. They've just discovered sellers with two suitcase nuclear bombs from Russia. They kill the sellers but find one bomb missing. It's been sold to someone and they must find out who has it, and fast. One of the dead men has a daughter who is involved in a science fair, and she may know to whom her father sold the second bomb. But it will take someone with more finesse to get the information from the girl. They go to their ace in the hole, Chesney Barrett, a recent recruit into their game of death. Chesney is an athlete, an Olympic swimming champion, and a biologist, plus she's sexy and beautiful. The story follows her as she infiltrates an ecological terrorist organization run by someone they think has the second bomb.

This exciting, action-packed story with fresh characters pulled me into the story from the beginning. I found it a little far-fetched that only this team and one lonely FBI agent are out looking for the terrorists when the whole alphabet soup agencies would have been put on the case if it was real. In fact, the FBI agent doesn't even know there's a nuclear bomb in the mix. The special team is the only ones who knows about the nuclear suitcase. The author's storytelling is superior, and the characters are topnotch, but there were so many wrong words page after page that it became a distraction. An editor or proofreader could have cleaned it up, and the author would have had a great book to present to readers. As it was, I had to knock it down to a 4-Star rating when it should have been a 5-Star novel. Still, highly recommended.

Tom Johnson, Author of *Nina Fontayne*

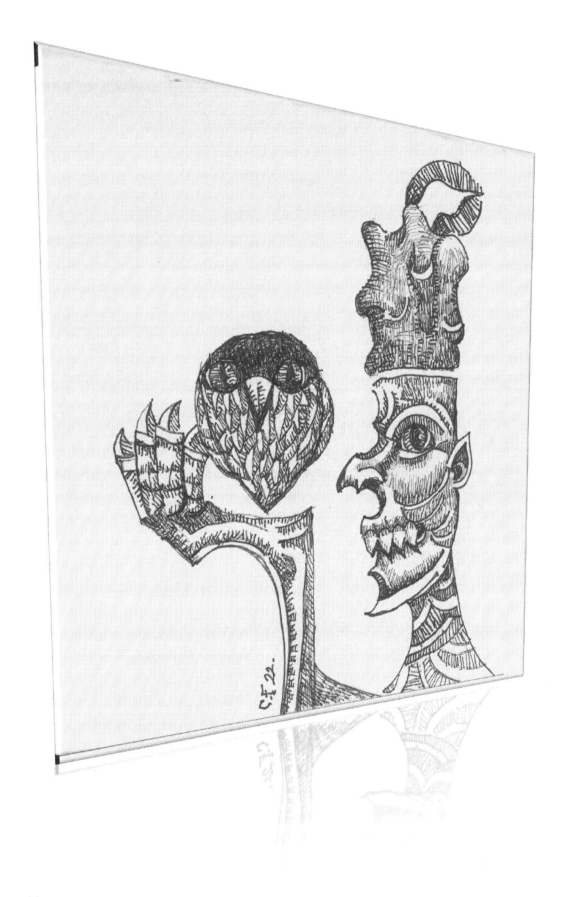

44

# His Darkness is My Light
## by
## Marge Simon

Born out of wedlock, a child of the streets, the sisters took me in to nurture and bequeath their divine formula. I was a willing novice, grateful for their care. Oh, I believed in the Word, the Truth, committed my life to selflessness, counting my rosaries on stone floors, a paper doll in a cardboard room.

Why can't I see the light in all this gloom? A key turns in the lock. I hear the creak of floorboards, —a shadow moves suddenly from the wall and joins my own. He materializes whispering my name. Ever so gently, he folds me in his cloak as his lips find my neck.

I hear them talking on the street, "Look at her face, see how she changed? Yes! Her brown eyes, bright with innocence, have turned dark as pitch. And see, where there once were tears are fresh tattoos—emblems of her Master, inked into her flesh. Scandalous, the way she flaunts her body!" Let them talk, let them wonder! I don't care.

I know the truth now, the truth that the sisters would never condone—his darkness is my light; I fly close beside him. We search out the sidewalk junkies, the castaways, the homeless victims, too proud for Salvation. We offer them comfort, freedom from this mortal life of hunger and pain in exchange for their souls, an offer they seldom refuse.

### The End

### Candlelighting by Lee Clark Zumpe

the match struck,
the wavering flame
spinning and flickering;
kissing the wick.

now a quiet glow settles over the chamber
breathing souls into shivering shadows
and sculpting life into the inanimate natives;

she comes to me in tenuous strands of mist
as soft as cascading moonlight
her murky eyes reflecting the dead of night.

she lingers through midnight
defying the ever-advancing day –
until the uninvited dawn
steals her from my embrace.

# The Quarantine Station
## by
## Lee Clark Zumpe

### 1. The Taint of Plague

At the time of my arrival in Smithville, I believed it safe to assume my ongoing affiliation with Dr. Herbert West had finally come to an end. I felt confident that the professional and social stigmata I suffered due to my relationship with West would soon pass and that I would gradually regain the respect and amity of my peers. Still, a part of me anticipated—and dreaded—the day West would arrive on my doorstep once more, zealously proposing to resume our research and revisit our investigations into that most morbid avenue of biochemistry.

Though West's perversions of science often nauseated me, my unrelenting intellectual inquisitiveness would forever enslave me to his advanced aptitude and tenacious resolve to press onward with this most distasteful work. His singular objective to reintroduce that vital spark into the mortal remains of the deceased at once fascinated and repelled me.

My assignment to the small, sleepy seaside village of Smithville had come as an indirect result of my past participation and support of West's early experimentation. An embarrassment to some, I found myself now impelled to follow the whims of academic administrators to win their approval. Dr. Alistair Malick, a senior faculty member at Miskatonic University in Arkham, had appointed me to lead the relief efforts in his hometown, where a fierce strain of smallpox had infected hundreds of fishermen and their families over a three-month period. The mission was two-fold: First, I was to provide medical assistance in treating the infected and stemming the further spread of the outbreak; and second, I was to monitor and record the unfolding events from a scientific standpoint, discovering the source and dissemination of the malady while documenting its progress and its limitations as a detached observer.

I embraced the undertaking as a personal and professional challenge, eager to demonstrate my willingness to partake in legitimate medical endeavors and apply my skills to benefit society. While I understood the gravity and the hazards of the situation, I felt myself well-equipped to carry out the mission.

Neither my educational background, which included an extensive exploration of various disfiguring ailments accentuated in grainy photographs and vivid, hand-colored illustrations collected in an assortment of descriptive textbooks; nor the awful events I beheld as a volunteer with the Canadians during the Great War; nor even the long string of unsettling, appalling, and, by most standards, unethical experiences I witnessed as West's accomplice could prepare me for the horrors I would face in Smithville.

Shortly after my arrival, I discerned that something more sinister than commonplace pestilence had afflicted the dwellers of seaside fishing cottages and the pallid, soft-spoken townsfolk who cowered behind locked doors. Even at its peak, the typhoid scourge that befell Arkham some 20 years earlier did not dispatch such great numbers with such speed, strength, and cruelty.

Smithville is a quiet North Carolina coastal community situated along the northern shore of the Kaldetseenee River, near where it empties into the Atlantic Ocean. Up the coast from Little River and southwest of the mouth of the Cape Fear River, the town was founded twice. Initially established in 1697, the settlement burned to the ground in the mid-18th century, only to be rebuilt in 1792. Unable to compete with Wilmington, the seaport accepted a less consequential and ambitious role in colonial commerce. Eventually, the harbor began attracting less reputable traders—those banned for various reasons from the major hubs along the Atlantic coast.

Exports included nothing more extraordinary than turpentine, rosin, tar, pitch, cotton, and peanuts. Imports, however, came from far-flung havens of questionable repute, with vessels arriving from Costa Rica, Capetown, Port Said, Tunis, Zanzibar, Durban, and Shanghai carrying contraband cargo, opiates, and spices, and on occasion, even more ghastly stowage. It was widely rumored that even now, well into the 20th century, ships ferried slave labor and indentured servants into the country for exploitation in coal mining, Appalachian logging camps, and other grueling drudgery.

It was reasonable to speculate that the smallpox had originated on one of these incoming merchant ships, had been introduced to the indigenous population through casual contact, and had developed into an epidemic because of a lack of proper diagnosis and corresponding preventive measures. Because of its isolation from surrounding communities and reliance upon a strict quarantine for all incoming vessels, Smithville had not recorded an episode of smallpox since the turn of the century. Unfortunately, this blessing made the town far more vulnerable to an outbreak since few members had developed life-long immunity. Smallpox—traditionally considered a childhood disease—could decimate a virgin population.

A tenth of the townsfolk had succumbed to the demon plague by the time I arrived, their fresh graves still awaiting tombstones in the old cemetery on the edge of town. Hundreds more had been infected and lay in various stages of infirmity, bodies defaced and identities obscured by blisters so densely clustered they overlapped. By day, the streets remained still and empty as the unaffected recoiled from all contact; by night, the village filled with the nightmarish shrieks of the sleepless tormented, trying ineffectually to distance themselves from constant agony.

My initial meeting with the mayor of Smithville was brief and awkward. Bertram Sellers' daughter had passed the previous evening. His wife was inconsolable and wept audibly in some far corner of his humble home. At my request, he provided me with ample documentation, including original copies of arriving ships' manifests. He also told me where I could locate the town's only surviving physician.

Sellers—a proud, religious man who earned the respect and admiration of his citizens—found it difficult to discuss the tragedy that had beset his community and his family. His voice frequently cracked during the interview, and stubborn tears hung from the corners of his eyes. He tried desperately to cloak his overwhelming grief, to remain at all cost in control and effectual as a leader as he described the chronology of events comprising the abominable epidemic.

The first signs of infection, he indicated, arrived in the form of severe muscle pain and great tenderness in the lower back and joints. Fever soon followed, and sometimes, death occurred before the telltale rash appeared. For the rest, the disease played out more slowly as the scarlet rash and tiny blisters annexed every bit of flesh across the body. The disease had initially appeared among the crews of pogie boats, spreading through the families of fishermen who lived in shacks and lean-tos in the marsh east of town. Sellers blamed them for bringing smallpox into Smithville.

He dismissed any suggestion that the disease had come into the town from arriving vessels, insisting that the quarantine had been rigorously enforced.

Though I still could not discount the possibility, I found no evidence in the records that there had been any breach or wholesale abandonment of Smithville's quarantine practices. Such a failure would have seemed peculiar since the town had been blessed with an elaborate offshore quarantine station by an unknown benefactor in the years following the Civil War—or, as the locals preferred, the War of Northern Aggression. This station, as viewed from the docks along the waterfront, had been built upon a shoal in Kaldetseenee Sound, about a quarter of the distance between Smithville and Lawley's Island. A sprawling complex set atop wood stilts, the station had its own water tower and infirmary, a kitchen capable of serving dozens of hungry sailors, a dockmaster's quarters, and a customs office.

Sellers assured me he had spoken with the station's chief attendant and physician, who swore he had seen no traces of smallpox in the weeks before the epidemic. All arriving vessels remained in quarantine for 15 days—long enough to detect any devious plague that might lurk among crewmembers, using them as ignorant hosts to gain a foothold in an untouched population.

Following my interview with the mayor, I visited the residence of the town doctor. I rapped on the door repeatedly, waiting for a reply. Though I thought I sensed shadows stirring behind the drawn curtains, and though I perceived the faintest hint of anxious whispers fluttering from hidden rooms down long corridors within the mansion, no answer ever came, and at length, I took my leave. I allowed myself the presumption that the doctor had been called away and that his responsibilities during the epidemic kept him out at all hours of the night and day.

Walking about the town, I found every store bolted, every government office closed, and every avenue vacant. The air was still and heavy, mournful at the scarcity of gentlemen's conversations, ladies' gossip and children's laughter. Smithville had become a ghost town, and as the light of day faded, a spectral mist crawled across Kaldetseenee Sound to haunt the abandoned wharves beneath dim lamplight.

I had stowed my belongings in a hostel overlooking the harbor. The innkeeper had attended to my needs apprehensively, clutching a kerchief to his face to check the spread of germs. I assured him I had been vaccinated years earlier and that I could not infect him, but his fear was insurmountable. I suspect he provided me with lodging only at the insistence of Mayor Sellers.

Before retiring to bed, I noticed an eerie glow piercing the fog outside my window — a dull ruddiness pulsing with hypnotic monotony, emanating approximately a quarter of the way between Smithville and Lawley's Island. I watched the flickering light for some time, weariness increasingly undermining my concentration until, at last, I fell asleep. At some point just before losing consciousness, I believe I witnessed a secondary source of light detach itself from the first, moving slowly toward the shore.

## 2. Amidst Freshly Dug Graves

I woke long before dawn and, finding myself rested, dressed and ventured out into the early morning twilight to walk the mist-shrouded streets of Smithville. The somnolent plague-sufferers, shunned by Morpheus and deprived of the luxuries of hibernation and dream, vented pitiable cries from their sickbeds where they wrestled with finding a moment's reprieve from constant torment. Their disheartening wails painted vibrant portraits of their malady, calling to mind the tiny, pus-filled blisters swarming over once gentle flesh, forever altering appearances and mercilessly scarring beauty.

On the outskirts of town, I made the first startling discovery of that day. A row of freshly dug graves crowned by temporary wooden markers provided an indication of the plague's most recent victims. A sparse scattering of flowers blanketed a few plots, though none boasted the fitting memorials seen in less perilous times. The lack of attendance and consideration grew from fear and panic, not callousness or apathy.

As a man of science, I had no tangible fear of loitering amongst the dead — at least, not under the current circumstances. Yet, as I strolled along the weedy avenues in that old cemetery beneath a sliver of the moon, I sensed a growing apprehension in my veins, an unsubstantiated accretion of juvenile fears I had not fallen victim to since that night in Boston when unspeakable things had transpired in the secret chamber beneath the tomb of the Averills.

I found myself scanning the shadows amidst mold-draped, centuries-old monuments, scrutinizing the copious and impenetrable pitch that always seems to accumulate in the last hours before the dawn arrives to wash away the ebon night. Perhaps the collective restlessness of the townsfolk infected my professional lucidity, or perhaps the half-buried memories of the consequences of my work with Dr. Herbert West resurfaced and culminated in an instant of frantic exasperation.

I cringed like a child at some unseen horror, frozen with fear and left clinging to the shadows at the base of an old oak at the very heart of the cemetery — a tree whose ancient arms stretched mightily to provide a gentle, leafy canopy to an ever-expanding necropolis.

Then, I saw them. Two lumbering figures came shambling out of the hedgerow toward the rear of the boneyard. Though one carried a torch, I could only roughly perceive their hideous, disease-ridden features across the distance. Both had been left mutilated by smallpox, with scars twisting and distorting their knotted, gristly faces into monstrous facades. Their long, brawny arms rippled with scabs and drained pustules and, even in the darkness, seemed tinged with a crimson taint.

In the eyes of one, the torchlight flickered — the reflected red radiance revealed only crude intimations of a base intellect, with no suggestion of individuality or emotive thought. On each forehead appeared an unnatural protrusion — a bulbous swelling encircled by bloody, inflamed tissue. So far removed, I could not identify the cause of this protuberance and wondered if it was an undocumented symptom of smallpox or a subtle sign the disease had developed into a new and more deadly incarnation.

With little consideration, the two unwieldy brutes selected a recently positioned grave and set about their depraved occupation. The sound of shovels thrusting earthward, violating both the soil and the sacred, conjured up images I had entombed years earlier and which I had hoped would nevermore see the light of day. Their present enterprise recalled that distant night when West and I had, by the light of oil and dark lanterns, set our spades in the unsettled loam of the potter's field and worked to uncover and liberate the contents of a recently placed pine box for our own dubious and selfish purposes. What followed in the black hours at the old Chapman place beyond Meadow Hill is history, if only recorded and evoked in our own secreted notes. It remains a blurry haze, an exercise that culminated in both success and failure — an undertaking resulting in equally profound academic exultation and moral deterioration.

I could not afford to lose myself in tenuous speculation or draw premature conclusions based on my biased perceptions corrupted by long-standing, salient fears. In all likelihood, the loathsome creatures engaged in the ghoulish act of unburying the dead were nothing more than common grave robbers, devoid of principles and desperate enough to disturb a victim of unspeakable pestilence for a few gold trinkets.

The two made fast work of it, accomplishing more in minutes than most would complete in an hour. I clearly remembered with shame the arduous, backbreaking task of grave digging — a charge I wish upon no man. It took West and me hours to secure our cadaver; yet, the scarred men of Smithville placed their hands on the intended corpse with dawn still an hour away. In the following moments, I ascertained they were not interested in filching the final possessions of the deceased — their objective was more complicated and gruesome than a simple theft of property.

After removing the body and depositing it into a canvas sack, they gathered their belongings, shoveled the displaced dirt back into place, and restored the gravesite to its previous appearance. Their meticulousness in returning the plot to its former condition contradicted their earlier haste in abducting the carcass and bordered on obsessive behavior. I watched with trepidation as they patted down the soil, straightened and tidied the marker, and placed dislocated blossoms on the ground with solemnity and considerable thoughtfulness. Their uncharacteristic concern suggested an intimacy with the deceased or a kinship of some unimaginable derivation and conflicted with their otherwise unemotional, disconnected malaise.

With dawn threatening to spill over the eastern horizon, the two corpse thieves retreated into the dense foliage at the precise point where they had first appeared at the edge of the cemetery, hauling their plunder into a tangled thicket of brush. Regaining my composure and once more incited to action by the same intellectual curiosity that had led me into dangerous and ethically ambiguous adventures, I felt pressed into an ill-conceived pursuit. Caution and prudence governed my initial footsteps, but I soon found myself speeding through the dense undergrowth, enveloped by darkness, scored and scratched by jagged twigs and thorny vines, striving earnestly not to stray from the poorly marked trail and to remain oblivious to those whom I trailed.

The rising, malodorous miasma around me and the sodden ground beneath my feet ensured me that I had ventured into the marshlands encircling the city, the very grounds from which Mayor Sellers believed the scourge had besieged Smithville. In the gloom, I perceived faint outlines—blackened silhouettes framed with straight lines and perpendicular angles, contours too tidy and seamless to be the work of nature. Though wholly obscured from identification, I guessed these hidden forms were scattered fishermen's hovels, dilapidated and aging huts wherein generations of seafaring families had been reared and raised.

I detected in my progress the moderate sloping of the soggy floor beneath my feet, falling toward the nearby water's edge. Dawn now lent an indistinct shimmer to the skies, an almost invisible radiance that spread across the gray firmament but failed to cast out shadows from the marsh.

A faint tang in the air which I realized I had unconsciously perceived at intervals since my arrival in Smithville became pithier and more pungent as I drew closer to Kaldetseenee Sound. The putrid odor reminded me initially of rancid corpses freshly plucked from the grave and half-devoured by ambitious worms. This stench, though, eclipsed even the reek of human putrescence with an overpowering and stomach-turning element of brine and sewage coupled with swamp vapors of the most deleterious fen imaginable.

Now, too, I noticed a disconcerting noise from every quarter. From the pools of pitch at my feet came an unnatural flip-flopping and smacking sound, along with an occasional pop and puff of air. The shadows betrayed only a hint of motion, so the source of the clatter remained veiled in darkness, patiently awaiting disclosure when the morning sun penetrated the dense marsh vegetation.

The tardy dawn found me on the edge of the marsh overlooking Kaldetseenee Sound. A rowboat slipped through the tides, pulling away from the shore with great haste and disappearing gradually into the folds of sea mist. Its occupants never looked back to notice they had been followed, never bothered to conceal the closing stages of their ghastly industry. On board, I saw the two brutes I watched earlier in the cemetery, the morning light now making their deformities even more evident. Between them, a slouched, canvas-covered corpse awaited some unfortunate fate inside the remote walls of the quarantine station.

Indeed, I did not have to guess the pathetic thing's future. I knew my old associate had taken up residence in that station and had recommenced tinkering with the edicts of nature. The morning light provided abundant evidence to establish his involvement.

The dawn had illuminated a grotesque assemblage of bony, decaying fish carcasses scattered across the marsh floor—each one clearly diseased and scored with lesions; each one half-eaten by waterfowl and dissected by insects and swamp vermin; each one long dead, netted weeks or months earlier by fishermen before the onset of the plague.

I stood in that awful graveyard, watching as the dead fish writhed and thrashed about against the muddy ground.

### 3. An Unanticipated Reunion

I spent the balance of the day assisting in treating the infected, helping the town's doctor provide medical assistance and reassuring his patients that the outbreak had already peaked and would soon recede—though I could not convince myself of that comfort. Fear I found in every face, young and old, wealthy and impoverished, pious and sinful. Unexpected and uninhibited disease often caused such despondency, introducing into the population it plagues the harsh veracity of uncompromising death. With explicit clarity, it illustrates the transience of our limited immortality and ultimately underscores the vulnerability of both the individual and the species.

Dr. Bryant Monroe Willetts welcomed my services and apologized for not making himself available the previous day. His experience with smallpox was limited, though his own immunity was assured due to a childhood bout with a less lethal strain. I found Willetts a competent man of medicine, somewhat old-fashioned in his diagnostic aptitude and approach to healing but refreshingly gracious, well-mannered, and unpretentious. His knowledge of folk remedies seemed limitless.

Willetts spoke highly of Mayor Sellers and his leadership throughout the epidemic, but his hesitation to answer my repeated inquiries regarding the quarantine station and its custodian—who he described as being "recently appointed with disputed credentials," assigned without his consent or endorsement—added to my compounding fears.

I spoke to no one about my suspicions. Had I informed the mayor, providing even a veiled glimpse as to the things potentially transpiring under the orchestration of my former scientific colleague, he would have labeled me a madman and dismissed me with a letter of disgust and censure that would have ruined my career. Only a handful of academicians comprehended the theories Dr. Herbert West proposed, and fewer still managed the courage to assign an ounce of confidence in them. To confess to anyone my first-hand familiarity with the processes by which reanimation might be achieved and to admit to both my complicity and my faith in successful experimentation supporting West's conjecture was tantamount to blasphemy in the eyes of my peers.

I decided I had to confront West, describe the nightmare he had somehow set into motion in Smithville, and induce him into considering the ramifications of his present line of research. As I tended to the victims of the scourge that afternoon, I tried to persuade myself that West was guilty of nothing more than criminal negligence, allowing the disease to burn its way through the weakest members of the isolated population until it waned, providing him with an abundant supply of fresh, albeit diseased, corpses for his experiments. I wanted to know that he had not unleashed the plague in the first place—that he had not allowed his obsession to replace compassion and culpability.

Late in the afternoon, I joined Mayor Sellers and his weeping wife at the edge of the old cemetery. They laid their daughter to rest in a freshly dug grave while a disillusioned pastor muttered a few utilitarian words to serve as a condensed tribute to the child's untimely passing. The preacher's listless eyes and unanimated sermon betrayed his inner turmoil, paralyzed by helplessness and questioning his own faith. I understood the betrayal he felt even though my academic background distanced me from his theological interpretation of the epidemic.

I had insisted that henceforth all victims should be cremated and that mortuary workers should be vaccinated to prevent further infections, and the mayor agreed to my request—but his wife would not allow it for their daughter. As she was lowered into the ground, I remembered her face from a family portrait I had seen in the Seller's parlor—young, fair-complexioned, a brimming smile that compressed all the wonder and innocence of childhood into a hopeful and optimistic moment lost to time. I had not seen her body after death, after the scourge left its hideous mark.

I hoped that she would rest undisturbed in the earth and that I would never chance to see the disfigurement both death and disease had wrought upon her. As we left the graveside, though, I felt greedy eyes fall upon the recently turned ground. Nightfall would soon arrive and instill West's minions with courage enough to do his bidding.

As dusk neared, I noticed a distinct change in the weather. The winds had increased, dispelling the fog which blanketed the harbor the previous evening. A cold gale swept the Carolina lowlands carrying legions of long, ragged gray clouds that grew increasingly menacing as they sailed across the sky. A black wall formed on the western horizon, swallowing the sun an hour before dusk and erupting in flashes of brilliant lightning that reached toward the Atlantic. Willetts had warned me he felt a storm coming, attributing his prophetic meteorological capacity to tender, aching joints and sinus inflammation.

With whitecaps crawling across the harbor as darkness descended, I made my way down to the neglected docks where it took little time to appropriate a rowboat that would suit my purposes. Light rain had begun to fall as I struggled against the wind, the surf, and the stubborn tide, determined not to allow the inconvenience of nature to obstruct me from the unanticipated reunion fated to take place that evening on the offshore quarantine station.

I barely managed to secure the rowboat to a floating dock at the station when the swollen storm-clouds overhead split and unleashed a brutal deluge that removed the little town of Smithville from view and made Kaldetseenee Sound seem as vast and unforgiving as the middle of the Atlantic Ocean. Rising waters inundated the dock as waves pounded the pilings and swamped my small ferry. Winds lashed the station with appalling ferocity and belligerence, and I scrambled up a nearby ladder in search of safety.

Two figures snatched me out of the weather, dragging me through the darkened halls of the quarantine station past empty cabins and rooms cluttered with laboratory equipment. I recognized much of the paraphernalia as stolen goods, long lost from classrooms at Miskatonic. The brutish forms which forcibly towed me deeper into the recesses of the station conveyed me in such a way that I could not see their faces; their much-maligned hands, however, were all too evident as they clutched my soggy clothing—their blistered flesh, crimson-hued and slick with rain-diluted pus, strained against tense and brittle bones while the disease continued to tear away tissues and corrupt vital internal organs.

And then there was West. Initially, he ignored my arrival, believing me to be no more than another corpse secured for what he believed to be his noble enterprise—his continued experiments into the reanimation of recently extinguished life. In those moments before he identified me—before he tore himself from his calculations and computations to study the prize his two underlings had delivered to him—I saw the same glut of conviction, the same elitist arrogance, the same narcissism that had shaped and warped his life's work. His genius was rivaled only by his madness.

When the spark of recognition finally distracted him from his intricate, convoluted calculations, he dismissed his contaminated toadies, relieved himself of his bloodied gloves and lab coat, and approached me with a genuine air of relief and congenial reminiscence. In those first moments, words proved too cumbersome to convey his delight at my presence. He approached and embraced me as though we were brothers connected by blood.

"What fortuitous favor brings my confidant and colleague to my side whenever the need is greatest," he said, and for an instant, I thought he might break down in tears. "Such providence lesser men may not acknowledge, but fate—defined as some cosmic engine driving the steady advance of science—has seen fit once more to align us on this ultramodern undertaking."

"Not this time," I said, interrupting his salutations. Though I fully intended to question him regarding the scourge that had beset picturesque Smithville; though I planned to reprimand him for conducting irresponsible experimentation responsible for adversely affecting the immediate environment, I already felt my resolve beginning to ebb, displaced as always by some uncontainable academic covetousness. "We must," I continued, "put an end to the suffering of these villagers."

"Yes, yes, of course." West, incurably overconfident, chronically smug, shrugged off my concern as if he had the power to end the affliction with the flick of a switch. "Everything will be fine. Only today I've completed work on upgrading a vaccine based on this new and virulent strain of the disease. Take it back to the town, inoculate the population." He directed me to a specific table in the lab upon which rested a wooden crate filled with vials of serum. "But the weather is far too treacherous to permit safe passage now. With sweeping tidal currents, the sound is difficult enough to navigate by day in the fairest weather. To set you off in these present conditions would be criminally careless." West knew he had a captive audience, knew he could count on my sympathies, knew he could convince me and implicate me in his deviant diversions. "Postpone your departure until morning. We have much to discuss."

## 4.  *From the Dark Water's Depths*

As the storm pummeled the exterior of the facility, I reacquainted myself with West as he provided a brief tour of the quarantine station, detailing the existing procedures adopted to prevent the kind of outbreak that was giving local grave diggers a grueling and strenuous season. The self-sufficient station boasted men's and women's barracks, a bathhouse, laundry, boiler house, disinfecting chamber, and crematory. While its design provided enviable efficiency and practicality, the Spartan accommodations felt drab and dreary and induced an intimidating sense of impotence and suppression.

The dispiriting atmosphere and aura of foreboding surrounding the fabricated island in the middle of Kaldetseenee Sound played perfectly into West's ambitions. His continuing studies demanded a certain clandestineness that in these prosperous years could not easily be obtained along the burgeoning Atlantic seaboard. The town, desperate for an educated physician not opposed to service in such an isolated outpost, had assured West that rarely would his services be required. Even during the busiest time of the year, only one ship a week utilized the disadvantaged port, opting to travel a few extra leagues to Wilmington.

Still, West's disreputable past created obstacles to obtaining any job, no matter how unpleasant, in his home country. Fortunately, he had made a modest fortune abroad in a series of recent pursuits he refused to describe in detail but which he referred to as "opprobrious, shameful, and sordid." Thus, his placement at the facility had been cinched by way of a substantial endowment made to the town's elders, an inducement that ensured both his tenure and his privacy. Their covenant apparently had been so lucrative that even though the epidemic coincided with West's arrival, neither Smithville's mayor nor its chief medical practitioner felt obliged to mention the correlation.

"I am not certain that the townsfolk are capable of deducing the cause-and-effect interrelation between the two events," West said, reaffirming his persistent tendency to disparage those with an academic deficiency. "But I will not deny the role I played in the unfolding of this tragedy, even though I could not have foreseen the repercussions of my well-intentioned deeds."

My silence coupled with an expression of incredulity disarmed the habitually stoic West, and, for a moment, he shed his gall and hubris and espoused a more conciliatory tone.

"How could I have imagined the series of events that led to this disaster? Even now, I cannot with any certainty point to the mechanism by which this malady was able to infect the residents of Smithville—I only know that my ambition, as always, clouded my judgment." His admission of guilt clearly taxed his fixed convictions. West, a man of unshakable principals, had finally confessed to being misguided by personal aspirations. "When we strive to achieve our dreams, we are sometimes blinded by the light of our own burning passions."

With that, West recounted all that had transpired, and together we tried to piece together the chain of lamentable misfortunes, mishaps, and missed opportunities that led to the execrable scourge. An aging schooner had arrived late one moonless evening, most of its crew either dead or dying. From the ravings of the surviving crewmen, West determined they had set sail from Loanda in Angola and that they carried with them contraband from the Belgian Congo.

Realizing that no one in Smithville had detected the arrival of the vessel, and knowing that he could not save the lives of the few remaining passengers, West made a reckless and inappropriate decision: He quarantined the doomed men in the station's barracks and then boarded the ship, carrying with him varying doses of a redesigned, refined elixir he believed could restore life to the deceased. Methodically, he injected the formula into each corpse he came across in the shadowy depths of the schooner.

He timed the experiment carefully, believing that if the reanimation of flesh were to occur, the serum would take no more than 60 minutes to facilitate the process. I cannot begin to imagine the excitement, the tension, and the anticipation he must have felt standing on the deck of that ship beneath the wary twilight, waiting to detect the faintest sounds of reinstated life wafting up from the cabin below. In his veins, too, running concurrently with that bloated expectancy flowed undiluted, unadulterated dread.

West could not predict how many corpses might respond to his treatment, could not divine the emotional attributes they might display upon meeting the orchestrator of their resurrection.

Not one came crawling into the starlight that dark evening, and West—acting on instinct—set the boat adrift on the outgoing tide long before dawn. Before disembarking, however, he started a fire in the hold. The doomed ship burned along the shoals where the harbor empties into the Atlantic.

As to the survivors, West possessed neither the time nor the resources to cure them, so he experimented on them even before the moment of death. Of the six, only two could be resuscitated after their hearts stopped beating, and these two had served him ever since. However, since their demeanor had been somewhat less than docile, West had been forced to relieve them of various bits of prefrontal cortex, extracted quite effectively through holes drilled in the forehead. Following the operation, he had inserted small corks in the opening of each man's skull, providing him with a decidedly expeditious method of destroying each reanimated servant should their behavior grow inauspicious. These plugs accounted for the unnatural protrusions I had observed the previous night.

Nothing in his tale, though, offered a direct link to the outbreak of smallpox in Smithville.

"Is it possible that someone onboard the schooner slipped by you and reached the shore?"

"Impossible," West said, pounding his fist on a tabletop in the station's central laboratory. The entire facility lurched under a barrage of undulating swells. The storm had churned up the dark waters of the sound transforming the usually tranquil harbor into a seething tumult. I wondered how the decades-old construction had been fortified to withstand such fierce weather—wondered how many such squalls it had already survived during its lifetime. West ignored the howling gale, the frothing seas, the roar of thunder and the relentless deluge that sent streams of water pouring through the threadbare roofing. His mind could not tear itself from the mystery at hand. "They were all too far gone. How they even managed to navigate the narrow passage into the sound I can't imagine."

"Yet, we both know somehow the disease reached the mainland." I gazed at the two reanimated brutes who had settled into quiescence in the corner of the room. "What about them? I spotted them in the cemetery last night, engaged in that despicable profession which once occupied us." I paused, hoping he would provide a logical explanation, hoping he could swear that their ghastly industry had a less terrible catalyst. "With the horrors the townsfolk already face, I would hate to think that you had so quickly surrendered to your scientific aspirations and resume experimentations before the outbreak had been contained."

"Of course," West answered, and I allowed myself to accept his response without further inquiry. "In this instance, I am free from reproach. The bodies I have collected enabled me to develop the vaccine that will end this nightmare."

"Perhaps, then," I said, still unable to determine the vector by which the contagion reached the nearby populace, "we should concede the fact that we may never know how this came to pass. Our energy would be better spent on seeing that every soul in Smithville is inoculated."

We concluded our discussion with this agreement. West, still concerned for my safety, led me to his private quarters and a comfortable bed. I initially refused his offer, not wanting to put him out; he, however, said he usually slept during the daylight hours and worked through the night.

Sleep came as the passing storms finally subsided. My dreams I found littered with disfigured faces, scarred survivors, and mourning parents gathered alongside hastily dug graves. West oversaw the grim calamity, detached and unresponsive, all but inaccessible upon his remote island. On and on he toiled, his dedication and determination so paramount that the peripheral consequences of his actions, no matter how significant, remained unnoticed. Though I believed in his vision and though I shared his dispassionate outlook, I could not pledge my services to him as I had often done in the past.

In the morning, I decided, I would return to the mainland to proceed with a meticulous vaccination agenda. Once completed, I would return to Miskatonic. My contribution to his research on this occasion would be my silence. I would not reveal his secret undertakings to the local authorities. I would not implicate his negligence as a source of the outbreak. I would report neither his whereabouts nor his illicit enterprise.

I had slept for several hours when the sound of a soft voice startled me. I lay on my side; my back was toward the doorway. I felt a gentle touch on my neck just beneath my ear, heard a woman's whisper as she leaned close to me.

"We must hurry. It is no longer safe here."

I turned toward the source of the admonition, but she was already halfway across the room. In the darkness, I could not make out her features. Her figure, though, appeared delicate and vaguely immature. She moved with the poise and grace of a patrician's ghost.

"Who is it?"

"Quickly," she said, her voice more determined now. She held out her hand, urging me to follow. "They're coming for him—they're coming to kill the reanimator."

All the lights throughout the station had been dimmed, and the corridors grew thick with the familiar stench of decomposing deep-sea creatures washed ashore following some tropical cyclone. The girl directed me through a labyrinth of passages until we emerged on the small floating dock where my rowboat awaited. Nearby, the wooden crate containing the vaccine had been stowed pending my departure.

"Take it. See to it that the town is saved."

Lingering clouds concealed the moon and stars, leaving only the lamplights along the waterfront to guide me. Then, for a moment, the heavens pierced the overcast skies and shed enough light to illuminate my immediate surroundings. Frightened, the girl backed away from me, fearing my reaction to her appearance. I immediately recognized her, recalling the family portrait in the Sellers' parlor.

"You're the mayor's daughter." Her alluring loveliness and striking features had been spared the ravages of physical deformity. Death must have come swiftly for her, a merciful end from an illness rarely known for clemency. In the shimmering twilight, I perceived the bluish tint painting her complexion, the paleness of her quivering lips, the eyes devoid of tears though sadness consumed her. In death, she remained the embodiment of elegance and beauty; in death, she offered irrefutable proof that West's theories were sound and that his methodology had evolved dramatically. I reached out and touched her cheek with the back of my hand. Beneath my caress, her face felt smooth and icy. "You remember everything, don't you?"

"Yes," she said, nodding. Sorrow poisoned her eyes. Though I could only guess the source of her anguish, I suspected that her chemically-induced restoration had somehow deprived her of something cherished and irreplaceable. In her suffering, I sensed that what West would claim as a miracle of science had, in fact, been an inexcusable curse. As if unseen gods acted to reaffirm my revelation, the dark waters of Kaldetseenee Sound stirred as creatures from the depths emerged. "You must go."

"What's happening?"

"They've come for him, all those he disposed of because their resuscitation took longer than he anticipated. All those he weighed down and tossed beneath the waves." I stared at the girl, shuddering, trying to envision the initial thoughts of those who awoke to find themselves fathoms deep. "My father knew what had transpired, and he did nothing. He knew if the townsfolk learned of the arrangement he had made, they would likely lynch him over it." Crawling out of the water, the revived dead shambled single-file into the quarantine station. Their bodies had been marred by disease, then further mutilated by ravenous sea fauna. Somehow, the disease had passed from these undersea lurkers into the local aquatic life. Fishermen caught the infected fish and consumed them, contracting the mutant strain of smallpox. "He's suffered enough, now—we've all suffered enough. Tonight, it ends."

Without another word, the girl turned and followed the macabre procession as it drifted inside the station. West must have known they were coming for him, must have prepared some kind of defense. Loyalty to my old colleague could not overcome my fear. I loaded the vaccine and set out for Smithville.

Before I even reached the docks, flames had engulfed the quarantine station. I heard sporadic gunfire, shouts, curses, and indescribable screams. As the situation deteriorated into relentless chaos, I realized that in all our noble endeavors, the closer we came to achieving the powers we ascribe to the gods of creation, the more intimate we became with the blind apathy and deleterious madness which most probably accompanies omnipotence.

Through the wanton manipulation of unobstructed science, Herbert West had all but emulated divinity only to find himself condemned by his own creation. I grieved that the world may have been deprived of his genius that night, though from his former miraculous escapes, I believe that any confidence in his demise is hollow.

As the morning sun began its slothful climb on the Atlantic horizon, a ribbon of smoke drifted south along the coastal flats of North Carolina, tied to the ruins of the quarantine station set a quarter of the way between Smithville and Lawley's Island. With no active fire brigade in town, the debris would smolder well into the day, leaving nothing more than a few charred pilings jutting from the dark waters where surging tides might trace tiny whirlpools in sea foam.

West had suggested some inconceivable alien design had repeatedly reunited us for the benefit of scientific advancement and, ultimately, for civilization and humanity. I could not help but wonder if such unnamed forces conspired to impede our progress and invalidate our innovations. Though as a man of science, I recognized the notion as implausible and immature—the thought of some cosmic counterbalance concealing cruel universal truths from the ill-equipped and unsuspecting eyes of mere mortals provided me with a satisfying sense of security.

Perhaps the pace of progress would slow for the balance of the century.

### *The End*

## Thing at the Window by Matthew Wilson

Someone had eaten the victim's face
In this old house where no one lived
But people whispered of the lights
Sometimes flashing in the little room.
My pistol was heavy in my hand
And the boy yelled when I opened the door
Exposing his macabre laboratory
Where his father roared in his chains
This thing that had been human.
I ordered it to freeze but it ignored my command
So I fired as it charged at me
Blowing its brain out the back of its head
Where it fell dead and twitching.
I called for backup to take the boy away
This poor soul who wished for revenge
On the man who had made his life a misery
But now his experiments have ruined more than him.
Soon that ugly place was demolished
Homeless strangers stopped vanishing
And for a while I had a peaceful town
Until there came a face at my window
The smile of the boy's mad and hungry mother
The chains that had once bound her to that laboratory wall
Glistened like ice in the moonlight
But not as bright as the knife in her hairy fist.
I grasped at my bedside table for the pistol
Firing at the breaking glass too late
For the thing at the window had found a new home
A quiet domicile to make a laboratory of her own
And I was her first experiment.

©2018 Doug E Marshall

61

# Tell Me I Don't Need to Know
## by
## Marc Shapiro

He had followed the show for years and seasons.

The blood, the entrails exploding at every turn, horror at its most base and adrenaline-charged obscenity. Equal parts H.P. Lovecraft, Mario Bava, and Clive Barker with a whole lot of bad intent thrown in for good measure.

Fred had literally lived and died by this sucker and, along the way, had become obsessed. When the show was on and the fangs and claws ripped and clawed as all matter of unearthly creations began their bloody wet work, Fred would enter a zone from which no interruption would be tolerated. Those around Fred and his world knew that for one hour, once a week, Fred did not exist except as a pair of eyes glued to the tube as all manner of horror leaped out of the screen and into his psyche.

It had gone on like this for years. Fred's woman knew when it was time to go into the other room and shut the door. No incoming calls would be allowed trespass and any that would sneak through the ramparts would be met by the wrath of somebody obsessed with the bloody and extreme. For that hour, Fred was not Fred, the hardworking, middle-class working stiff who shuffled through his days and nights as a white-bread society submissive to the system. Fred, at that moment, was the junkie whose inner demons were satiated by a show about extreme horror in all its bloody red shades.

But as his TV drug rounded into the clubhouse turn of hiatus and a much-trumpeted final six episodes that would provide answers and the ultimate reason why he had stuck it out to the bitter end, things began to unravel in Fred's world.

And real horror, not Hollywood horror, came to call.

Fred's wife took sick and quickly deteriorated. Fred loved his wife in the best possible way and took the time-honored mantra of "In sickness and in health" seriously. Health had been a breeze. Sickness was the real-world horror show. No sleep. Constantly checking her oxygen levels. Helping her on and off the toilet when her body cried out for help. Trying to get her to eat. Watching helplessly as she wasted away in body and spirit.

One day the Grim Reaper came to call. Pure and simple, her heart stopped. The EMTs did their best as Fred stood and watched them work on her as they transported her to the hospital. Where a doctor came out of an emergency room anti-chamber and delivered the bad news. Fifty years and gone. No words on the written page. No actor struggling for his motivation. No well-placed commercial where corporate America is trying to get their hands on your wallet.

This is absolute horror. The kind of stuff fake horror can't hold a candle to.

And the nightmare rolled on. Called the mortuary. Arranged for cremation. A quiet last moment where Fred saw her body lying in peaceful repose in a quiet room. He kissed her on the forehead. One last kiss as the tears began to fall.

Fade out. No happy ending. Hollywood does Hollywood. The real world runs on a different schedule.

Fred continued to live with the memories and the horror of real life, paying scant attention to the notices that his favorite slice-and-dice series was about to come back on the air. Fred knew it was coming, but he did not care anymore.

But old habits died hard.

On the night his show began airing the first of the final countdown episodes, Fred slouched into his chair and stared at the screen. At the appointed hour, Fred reached for the remote, pointed it at the screen, and pantomimed clicking it on.

Fred dropped the remote on the floor and stared at the blackness. His eyes glazed over. Everything that had brought him to extreme horror had been washed away by life. Tears ran down his cheek as he recalled the real horror of his life. Fred knew the real horror, the loneliness, the sadness, the helplessness, and the memories of real horror that ran cold and black.

Fred had no desire to find out how his show ended. He knew real horror and that real horror never goes away.

## *The End*

## The Resurrection of Mia by Sandy DeLuca

Thunder...
a flash of light across
a pitch-black horizon.
Biagio kneeled on Mia's grave.

Slight wave of his hand,
a look to that dark sky—
moonless, starless—
rain pouring down.
Howl reverberated...
through night.

He dug,
into soft, wet dirt...
quickly,
preternaturally.

At last,
body uncovered,
he reached down, lifted it.

Such a delicate, old woman—
pure white hair,
wrinkled flesh,

hands and feet bony...
raw.

"Mia," he whispered...
I've never done this for a woman."

He kissed her lips,
almost tenderly...
a fingernail across her neck.
Deep into flesh,
until blood flowed.

A drop on his tongue...

Not dead long—
less than an hour,
but a bitter taste lingered.

*I have to try.*

Rain poured down,
soaking him.
So, he drank swiftly.

Next,
he reached for a dagger...
cut his palm,
flinching a bit.

He lowered his hand,
Brushed it over Mia's lips,
saying, "Taste my blood. Be alive.
Be young again.
By the power of darkness—
I command you to rise from the curse of death..."

Yet, her body remained still,
and he whimpered softly,
efforts in vain.

"Live, I command you,"
he bayed into rain and wind.

Soon, soft moaning erupted.
A stream of mist spiraled from her lips.
A whoosh of wind emerged—

twisting, burrowing leaves and sticks.

In the distance,
ocean waves crashed with fury
and the cries of restless seabirds echoed.

Mist floated from her fragile form—
from her chest, her hands,
her torso.
Thick, white, like phantoms...
shrouding the old body at first,
gradually dissipating.

He watched with fascination
as slowly,
elegantly,
Mia's skin began to smooth,
hair shifted from white
to a seductive shade of red.
Mud and dirt fell from her flesh...
her clothing.
The sagging, scrawny form became full...
voluptuous...
beauty shone as it did when they first met...
for a moment, emotion welled...
But he'd have no part of human weakness...
swore it off centuries before.

So, he commanded, "Rise, Mia?"

She opened her eyes,
brilliant green,
lips red.
And she said in a guttural tone,
"I was sleeping, dreaming.
I floated away..."
She rubbed her forehead,
"Damn, everything hurts.
Why'd you bring me back?"

"The pain will go away...
I promise."
He opened his mouth,
revealing sharp fangs
and he growled,

"I've resurrected you—
made you an immortal—
I'm your master.
And I love you in my own way."

She wrinkled her nose...
"Oh, stop with the drama.
Told you a million times,
it's not love.
It's your pride.
I guess it's true
that you revived me...
your blood...
and mine mingled.
But remember everything goes full circle...
and you may have created your own demise."

He threw back his head,
laughed...
"Nothing can destroy me.
I've been here for centuries."

She smiled shrewdly...
"Lots of things have been here for centuries...
doesn't mean they can't be ruined."

He pointed a finger...
"Be a queen of night...
*my* queen."

"Oh, for hell's sake,
you and over the top dramatics,"
she hissed.
"I'm leaving you...
don't try to follow..."

He answered softly,
"You always leave me
and I may regret this...
but go..."

And she floated away,
over the trees,
rooftops,
steeples,

and the restless sea...
singing an old lullaby...
one of horror and death.

In time he'd follow...
maybe one night
he'd send her back to her dreams...
But for now, he watched her slight
body bend and soar within the storm...
white skin like the spirit moon
cruelty in her heart...
beautiful...
deadly.

## The Vampire in His Eyes by Hillary Lyon

the full moon rises
as do the wind and the clouds

of fog swirling
around her bare feet

as she stumble-dances
through her sleep-

walking, wandering
through the maze

of her haunted mind
she follows the flickering

promise of love
in the midnight embrace

of her darling's darkly shining eyes
luring her to the end of this dream

where he waits patient, handsome,
and hungry

# Crosses of Cold Castles
## (For Charles Perrault)
## by
## Matthew Wilson

Dad said that for the good of the kingdom, I had to marry his enemy's daughter. He couldn't lose any more soldiers in a failing war, so I said yes, but only after he swung me round the room by my hair.

Julie's handshake was cold and crushed my fingers, but I feared the honeymoon because of the black sockets where her eyes should have been. Only dark holes remained in her grinning skull, and what became of them, I don't know.

I had nightmares about her eyeless sockets, like a pocket of space where stars went to die.

I was to marry and have children with her? What if they inherited her fangs and pale white skin?

"Welcome to my castle, Prince John." She smiled with sharp teeth when the fanfare died down, but she only showed me the door when we were alone.

"This is to be your home now, but I have one rule—NEVER go in there."

I nodded but knew I'd try to get in there the first chance I got.

Her caresses chilled me, and her kisses burnt me in the dead of night. When sleep would not come, my thoughts returned to the little door down the hallway.

"Julie?"

How could you tell a woman without eyes was sleeping? Her breathing seemed regular, and when I called her name again with no reply, I moved so slowly that the seasons might change quicker.

When I was out of bed and dressed, I headed to the little room.

Locked.

I rooted many hours for a key to unlock it, wrestling with my thoughts that the secrets beyond didn't matter. Dad had told me not to make waves, to marry someone I knew nothing about for the sake of peace.

But that little door would not leave my head.

"I awoke alone last night," Julie pondered at dinner the following evening, though I never saw her eat. "I didn't hear you come to bed."

"Just nerves," I lied and wondered if those dark spots for eyes could see through my deceit. My heart was racing. "Do you only move about at night?"

Julie didn't have a plate but squeezed the knife in her hand. "I don't like the sun," she said. "I don't want us to have secrets, John—a good marriage is built on trust."

Of course, I told her everything was fine, that I was adjusting to the switch from my home to hers. But when she went about her business, I gave myself a stitch running about a house that still didn't feel like my own in pursuit of the key.

It was in the chimney, suspended several feet up the flume on a ledge so I had to get soot on my boots while clambering up there. No doubt there had to be something important in that room with all the effort of hiding a key—maybe attack plans on Father's kingdom. Maybe this was a sham marriage to lower his defences.

Then when Father was dozing on celebratory wine, the missiles would fall, and evil would win.

My feet echoed too loud on the stone corridor and my heart threatened to drum out of my chest when I opened the door. I swung it open—and there they were.

Father had kept me from the battlefields, so the twelve pale men chained to the wall made the world swirl around me. I gagged and nearly passed out.

Were these prisoners? Surely no crime was worth such cruelty.

One noticed me and reached out for help.

"Cru - crucifix," he gasped.

Was he delirious and seeing things? Did he want me to scoop up some dropped memento so he could die in peace? I looked at the floor and saw nothing, but then I heard it—the scraping at the window. It sounded like a wild animal snorting.

I knew I had to hide and threw myself against the wall, clutching chains around me, and any monster not consumed by bloodlust would have taken a moment to realise there were thirteen almost dead princes in that room instead of twelve.

Foul-scented smoke filled the room, and when it collected into a form in the moonlight, I recognised my bride, the grinning thing whose heels clacked against the stones as she detected movement.

"Oh, you still have some fight?" Julie asked. "Do you have something else for me?"

The prince went limp as she folded herself around him, biting at his neck. I think I heard my chains rattle, telling myself to stop shivering out of fear she might hear me.

Slowly, awfully the feast was over, and the prince went limp.

Julie wiped her mouth and walked to the window, stopping only momentarily as I suppose she had caught a sound.

*Slow your heart,* I thought. *Smooth your breathing.*

Julie shrugged and threw herself back out the window like she meant to end her life, but I heard no distant shriek, no sound of impact.

God, the woman I was married to was a monster.

I had to get upstairs before she realised I was away.

"S-stop shaking," I told my hands as I ran out of the room, but when I turned the key in the lock, it snapped.

I tasted vomit again as my finger stabbed at the bit of steel stuck there—my digit bled, but I couldn't get it out—the key was broken in half, and now she would know.

Would she lock me in that awful room with the rest of her victims?

She had come through the window like a spirit—did she use the door at all? Maybe she would never notice.

But when she tried to murder me later, it was obvious that she had.

**\*\*\*\***

Dreams are a terrible thing in an ebon castle. Again, I heard those poor chained men calling, begging for help, and I had abandoned them, fleeing with my tail between my legs like a coward.

What kind of king would I make? I was not worthy of a throne or my father's name — I could hear the men wail even when I was awake, shaking and sweating. I didn't know if it was real or in my head.

I only knew that I had to go back.

It was nearly morning, and Julie was sleeping when I left her. The night bird seemingly only lived for the night, and I hoped I had many hours to do what I meant — to be the son worthy of a king.

The cobweb-covered prisoner I had abandoned had called for a crucifix, so I took the one my mother had given to me on parting for protection. Maybe it would rouse the poor fellow.

The door was closed as I had left it and creaked too loudly as I gritted my teeth and swung it open. A rush of cold air stung me from the window, but I could not run away from the chance of redemption.

Besides a gurgle, the men with broken crowns might have been dead for all I knew, but I had a hacksaw in one hand and frantically started sawing at the nearest chains.

"John?"

I heard a clang and realised I had dropped my only weapon when I turned and saw the figure at the door.

"What are you doing?" Julie said, very aware of what I was up to. "I don't normally stay up this hour, but the racket you're making with that saw would wake the dead."

"What am I doing?" Fear gave gas to my anger. "How could you do this? Treat people like this?"

Julie advanced into the little room, and my body forgot the sensation of cold.

"They're not people," she corrected. "They're my food."

Again, I marvelled at her movement; even without eyes, she stepped without a stumble around the half-masticated men. Her smile was too wide; her teeth were too big.

I shrieked as I imagined those fangs around my throat and fell back against the window — it was a long way down, and so I didn't dare look outside, but Julie stopped when she did.

"Come here, John. I'm not mad that you didn't listen to me. I only want to talk."

She clicked her long nails excitedly like a crab cutting up a small fish with its claws.

Then I realised I was in the light of the rising sun. It wasn't far above the distant mountains, but the crown of it was throwing light on the walls.

*I don't like the sun,* she had told me.

"I - I'm happy enough here," I said, and for an hour, we faced each other off. She shuffled backward as the rays of the strengthening sun reached across the floor.

"My father shall hear of this madness," I said. "He shall bring his cannons and —"

"Your father shall hear nothing," Julie insisted. "Night always comes, and when it does, you shall join these fools who said no to me."

With a huff, she turned and slammed the door shut behind her, taking the head of the nearest prince to vent her fury on.

So was this how I died? To become a monster like her, forced to feed on flesh to stave off the hunger pains? I refused to give my soul so simply. Maybe a moment's bravery in throwing myself to the rocks below would end my suffering?

No, what had become of the king I was supposed to be? My body wanted to vomit up my skeleton, but if I couldn't handle one thing pretending to be human, then I deserved death.

Eventually, it would be night. Would I hear those claws at the window again? There was no glass — no protection.

"Cru- crucifix," someone called, and I recognised the dry and wheezy voice as the prince I had abandoned earlier. He lived and my heart felt light for it.

"Here," I said, removing it from the chain on my neck and pressing it into his hand. "I didn't forget it," But despite his dehydration, he had strength; he refused to accept the gift like an ungrateful child at Christmas. He thrust it back at me.

And then the door exploded.

I was so intent on running to the voice, to not be alone in that awful place that I didn't realise the other prince was out of the sun until my soul felt cold. I was about a foot out of reach of the rays when Julie saw her chance.

"Not smart for a prince," she said as her hand went around my throat. She squeezed, uninterested in my final words. "How did your father win all those battles without teaching his son about distractions?"

She stopped talking when her face started melting when I pushed the crucifix in my hand against her jaws to keep those teeth away. I heard a hissing, registered a reek of cooked flesh, and finally breathed again as I fell, dropping like a stone onto my rump as Julie staggered backward.

Into the sunlight.

I reached for her as her hair caught fire like yellow snakes spitting at me, but when she flashed her claws at me, I fell away and clutched the shallow cut in my elbow.

Her dress rippled, trying to contain the rush of hot air beneath and then went up like lit paper. Her bones broke, trying to reform, and surrendered to the heat of the sun like fireworks. Within moments, she was ash, and only I and a few half-living men remained in that cramped and cruel room.

A month later, I had that castle destroyed. I didn't tell Father what happened and paid off the contractors who found thousands of bones beneath its foundation.

Yes, it was terrible how the plague was common and had taken away my new bride, but I had married Julie to stop the war. Her father would rain down hell if he knew what I had done to his daughter.

Yes, sir, I loved your daughter. I cared for her and destroyed her castle because I couldn't deal with the memories of her death.

My own father was less forgiving, as his greatest enemy had no reason NOT to attack his gates. In the future, there might have been a child between Julie and I that ruled both kingdoms, and the eastern king would have secured his future with peaceful means.

Now there was no reason to stay his hand.

That is why my father beat me, pulled my hair, and threatened a great torture on me.

That is why I married Julie's younger sister, who also hated the sun.

Although this time, she had eyes, at least, the eyes of wolves that chilled my blood.

The wedding was another charmed affair that pleased all but me and surprisingly took place at night. I had thought the whole family monsters that the sun destroyed, but Karla loved the hot rays. She bathed and danced in them.

Honestly, I don't know if there is any way to kill this princess.

Or our snouted pups that love the forest.

### *The End*

## Vlad's Lament by Marge Simon

Daylight Savings
A vampire's dream
Though it ends
After Halloween.

But when it stops,
(A peeve of mine)
So much to drink
In much less time.

I speak for my kind,
And we're irate
We won't accept
This be our fate.

The sun won't rise
Let's make it clear
Until we say so
every year.

74

# The Rose
## by
## Rod Marsden

Joan, in her thirties and well-dressed, found herself with a solemn task. With a white rose in hand, she knocked on Kat's door. Kat came to the door, wondering who could be calling. It was mid-afternoon on a sunny day in September. There was a tree shading Kat's modest Wollongong home and, in that tree, sang a noisy minor with its grey feathers and yellow face mask. Kat was in her early seventies and not used to young visitors.

"Are you Kat Morris?" asked Joan. "I mean Syd's Kat?"

Kat looked Joan up and down and said, "My name is Katrina Morris and I don't belong to anyone. I know Syd Jenkins. We have been friends, a long time now. But I certainly don't belong to him. Who are you?"

"I'm Joan," replied the younger woman, looking down. "Syd's my uncle."

"How is Syd?" asked Kat. "I haven't seen him in a while."

"He passed away recently," said Joan, looking at her shoes.

"That's so sad," reflected Kat. "We had some good times together. What can I do for you?"

Joan cleared her throat and presented the flower. "Syd was my uncle and, in his will, he wanted me to give you this."

"A rose?" wondered Kat.

"He specified it should be a white rose," added Joan, handing the rose to Kat, who took it. She smelled the rose.

"It's a commercial rose from a shop." Joan sighed. "No doubt grown in a greenhouse. So, it doesn't have much of a scent."

"But why a rose?" asked Kat. "Why a white rose? And why give it to me?"

"I don't know." Joan shook her head sadly. "Syd died of cancer. He was my uncle. I want to do right by him. What was he to you, if I may ask? The rose must mean something."

"He was a friend," Kat told her. "As to what the rose means. I haven't a clue. Do come in. Where are my manners? I shouldn't leave you standing at my doorstep like this."

Kat led Joan to a sitting room with sofas, large armchairs, and an enormous television screen. There were also books on shelves and a little yellow canary in a cage. Kat offered Joan a chair, and she sat. She then told Joan she would make some tea for them and headed for her kitchen. Sometime later, she returned with steaming cups filled with Earl Grey. She still had the rose in her hand.

Joan took the tea offered and asked, "Did Syd love you?"

"I suppose so," replied Kat, "but we were just friends."

"Are you sure?" asked Joan, after sipping some tea.

"Yes, I'm sure," said Kat emphatically. "Between the two of us, I am sure we can work this out."

Unbeknown to both women, the spectre of Syd Jenkins entered Kat's home and hovered over his loved ones. Neither Kat nor Joan could see him, which was the way he wanted it to be.

"The rose stands for purity," Syd told himself. "I, Sydney Jenkins, was not the bad boy, Kat, you wanted. No, not the bad boy at all."

"I think, at one stage, Syd may have been infatuated with me," confessed Kat after taking a sip of tea. She rested the cup on a small glass-topped coffee table.

"Oh, I was! I was!" bleated Syd, who could not be heard.

"I went out with him anyway," said Kat.

"I was lumbered with the name Sydney," moaned Syd's spectre, circling the room in a frenzy of waving arms. "Aaaghhh! What were my parents thinking? How many times has the name Sydney been used for a dropkick in some movie? Syd, I suppose, is fine. I pushed for more of a life with you, Kat. You said no, and we left it like that."

"Syd and I went out many times," informed Kat. "But we were never intimate, not in a physical sort of way."

"Why not?" asked Joan after finishing her tea and putting her cup beside the other one on the coffee table. "I mean, in a physical sort of way."

Kat shrugged and said, "He just wasn't my type, but I did like his company."

"What type is that?" wondered Joan.

"Adventurous!" revealed Kat.

"But I went on adventures with you!" cried Syd to himself. "Don't you remember?"

"He wasn't wild, if that's what you mean," said Joan. "He was quiet. He had his photography. So why did you spend time with him?"

"He knew the south coast of New South Wales better than I did," mused Kat. "He could point to architectural wonders I wasn't aware of. Also, he had a good sense of humour."

"I know he wasn't the sporty type." Joan sighed.

"That's not quite right!" cried Syd, still not to be heard. "I jogged, and I played squash with you, Kat. I just didn't follow footy on tele."

"In college, he took up fencing," said Kat. She smiled at some long-ago memory.

"Was he any good?" asked Joan.

The spectral Syd found he had a foil in hand and could flourish it about. "I was Errol Flynn reborn!" he shouted to himself. "Take that, you villain! And that! And that!"

"He was all right," replied Kat. The foil in Syd's hand then disappeared.

"Was he much into gardening or symbolism?" asked Joan.

"I dabbled in symbolism." said Syd.

"Was he into gardening, you ask?" said Kat, waving about the rose. "No. But I do recall him telling me about *Born in Blood*, a book he once read about Freemasonry. Also, *The Da Vinci Code*."

"Anything else?" asked Joan.

"He was into medieval heraldry." Kat smiled knowingly.

"There!" cried Syd. "You have your clue."

"The rose can't have anything to do with dancing," mused Kat after a moment's thought. "He hated disco."

"I took up ballroom dance, in my later years," disclosed Syd to no one but himself.

"You really don't know why it should be a white rose?" asked Joan.

"The rose was used in medieval heraldry," said Kat. "The white rose was the symbol of York in the War of the Roses, or that's what Syd once told me."

"That was twenty years ago!" cried Syd. "I can't believe you remembered."

"So, the white rose stands for York," said Joan. "Then my uncle was a Yorkist? And you, too, are a Yorkist? And you were Yorkists together! Now we are getting somewhere."

"We are?" wondered Kat.

"Ta, da!" cried Joan with a hand sweep, as if she had a sword in hand. "Bring up the cannon. Archers at the ready. Bring on the cavalry. On to victory!"

"Blast those rotten Lancastrians with their red roses," shouted Kat. "Blast them to Hell and back. We're Yorkists!"

"Really?" wondered Joan.

"No, I don't think so," murmured Kat. "Medieval history and heraldry were his thing, my dear, not mine."

"Could you be Yorkist royalty, tucked away in Australia?" asked Joan.

"No!" cried Kat. "And Syd wasn't of noble birth either. He would have told me if it was so."

"But he would have liked to have been?" asked Joan.

"I suppose so," reflected Kat after looking more closely at the rose she held. "Yes, yes! I'm sure of it. I think he would have fancied himself a knight."

"So, this rose is a final knight's gesture to one fair maiden then?" enquired Joan.

"No, not so fair, I'm afraid," replied Kat, shaking her head. "I have been married and divorced. I have children, all grown up now."

"But fair in his eyes?" asked Joan.

"That would be ever so strange," contemplated Kat. "But that could be true."

"It's true!" cried Syd.

"I think we have figured out the rose," revealed Kat, sounding satisfied.

"I agree," said Joan. "You are a maiden. He is a knight. It fits."

Joan stood up and curtsied before Kat and added, "I should have gestured so and said Milady when I offered you the rose."

"Too late now!" said Kat, waving the rose at Joan. "I already have it. And thank you again for Syd's gift to me."

"You're welcome," replied Joan, sitting down again. "And Syd would say you are welcome too."

"Yes, I would," said Syd emphatically.

"So, a knight's final gesture?" wondered Kat, waving about the rose.

"That's not what I had in mind, but it will do," Syd told no one. "I feel rather heroic. A little too noble for my own good, I will grant you, but there you have it. And so, I say farewell to both of you. The rose is in good hands."

Syd bowed to first Kat and then Joan before making his way to and through the front door. He was off to where spirits go when their business on earth is concluded. He had a happy departure.

"Want to get a drink somewhere in memory of Syd?" ventured Joan.

"Sure, why not?" shrugged Kat.

"What do knights drink?" asked Joan.

"A tankard of ale?" ventured Kat.

"And what do you suppose maidens drink?" wondered Joan.

"Wine," said Kat. "But I'm not much of a wine drinker."

"Neither am I," confessed Joan. "A tankard of ale, in memory of a friend, would suit the occasion nicely, don't you think, Milady?"

"I agree," said Kat. "Do you reckon they have tankards at the local pub?"

"Let's find out!" cried Joan.

Both Kat and Joan got to their feet and left Kat's home for the nearest pub, which had schooners instead of tankards. They toasted to Syd, wishing him well in the afterlife. The rose was now on the table beside them.

## *The End*

## The Night Dancer by Matthew Wilson

Against Mother's advice I took the shortcut
Stopping dead when the girl called out to me
That woods were no place for intruders
Who should have listened to local history.

Her burning eager eyes robbed my strength
Her kiss whispered not to be afraid
As she took my hand and walked forward
To her victims buried in the glade.

In the pregnant moonlight we danced
Sipping wine within this ebon dell
The bloodied goblet rolled my head
Her promises damned my soul to hell.

With the dawn the spell was broken
Light burned darkness from the land
When I blinked and realized she was gone
With only her cape there in my hand.

# Duppy
## by
## *Rajeev Bhargava*

Yet another bloody, mutilated, and gruesome murder victim had been discovered by LIT, whose abbreviations stood for the Law Investigation Team. It was headed by Detective Fuji Yamaha, a robust man in his mid-thirties with a paralysed left leg. The scene of the murder posed a riddle.

Gory, disturbing, and difficult to investigate, bloodied and mutilated body parts were planted neatly across the network of paths and hedges, which made up the sections of a massive *Maze of Phantom Spectres*, located in a Funhouse Theme Park.

Just then, Detective Fuji's mobile phone sounded its familiar bell tone. It was a text message that read:

*"The fun has only just started. Enjoy the show! ~ **Duppy**."*

"'The Maze Serial Killer' had just announced his arrival." Detective Fuji turned to one of his team members, a young lady in her twenties. "Ms. Stobo, I want this place closed to the public immediately."

The body was soon identified as that of a teenage girl aged eighteen, named Sarah Pastel, the elder daughter of Henry Pastel, a retired art lecturer who now ran his own business, a shop named *Pastel's Portraits*. Now in his late sixties, he hoped to hand over his business to Sarah, a budding artist, until her murder. Henry was left in complete shock and disbelief.

"No, I can't accept Sarah could just leave me this way. Impossible. I need to go out and look for her." He suffered from various health problems, which included arthritis, so his walk was slow and painful. Nonetheless, life moved on, and he had to make a living. He headed for the door, about to revert the "Open" sign to "Close," then leave when he felt a warm hug around his waist. It was Bertha, his younger daughter, who was just thirteen.

"Oh, Daddy." Henry turned to see her. Her eyes appeared so calm and angelic.

He stroked her medium-length auburn hair softly. Then his expression changed, and he said aloud, "Bertha, don't stop me now. I have to go and look for your sister. Aren't you the slightest bit concerned for her welfare?"

"Daddy, you know I am. She was my sister."

"Listen to me, Bertha. Those remains were *not* Sarah's."

Just then, the door opened, and Detective Fuji entered. He removed his hat and bowed his head. "I'm sorry, Mr. Henry, but the decapitated blood-soaked head was that of your daughter, Sarah. I'm afraid I'm going to have to order you to remain here for your own safety. This is a private case involving a serial killer. I've taken the liberty of placing police guards around your shop. I assume you and your daughter live here." He turned to Bertha.

"And it was you, wasn't it, Bertha, who identified her." She nodded.

Just then, Detective Fuji's eyes fell to the floorboards. "I can see one of your customers had extra-large feet."

They all stared at them.

"Dad!" called out Bertha. "I never noticed anyone come in since morning."

Detective Fuji grimaced and scratched his chin. "Do you have a logbook where you record all the customers who come in?"

"Of course!" cried Bertha. "Closed-circuit television-. We can check it. It's in my room."

He smiled.

"Listen, I admire an intelligent young lady. Thank you, but I must emphasise that this is a private investigation, so I need to work only with my team on this case, strictly on duty. Now, if you don't mind, I'll contact my colleague."

"No, of course not. Please go ahead," said Henry. He put his hands into his daughter's reassuringly and said softly: "It's all right, darling. Let them do their work. We just need to cooperate."

Detective Fuji spoke on his mobile.

"Ms. Stobo, it's all right, you can come in now. I need you to help me operate the CCTV."

"I'm in the back of the shop, you idiot!" replied a hoarse voice. Then the phone disconnected.

"How strange. She never spoke to me like that before."

There was a moment's silence, and then Detective Fuji's eyes filled with fear. He turned to the others.

"Where's the back exit?"

"This way," replied Bertha and led the way.

Outside, he looked around frantically and saw a smashed-up mobile phone.

"Ms. Stobo! Where are you?"

"Aaaahhhhh!" screamed Bertha. Detective Fuji turned and headed towards her. She was staring at a pool of blood where a skinned and stout lady sat crouched, covering her face.

"Ms. Stobo … is … that you?"

She looked up at him to reveal a mauled face with eyeballs popped out, after which the semi-living corpse sang:

*"La la la la laa, he's out to get you*
*And is on the prowl tonight,*
*Terrifying all that come in his path*
*Better to lock your windows and doors tonight*
*Coz' Duppy's coming to get you. La la la laa laa."*

After that, her body slumped sideways, lifeless into a heap, like a contorted doll. Bertha looked away, sickened, while Inspector Fuji removed his hat, bowed his head, then removed his coat and covered the body.

He then contacted Headquarters.

"Hello, this is Detective Fuji. This is an emergency. I want a couple of police officers here right away. It's at *Pastel's Portraits*, a corner shop, first turn from the Funhouse Theme Park. There's also a body here. I want a postmortem performed immediately."

He then turned to Bertha and looked at her seriously. "Bertha, it's not safe for you and your father to remain here alone. You need police protection."

He shifted his gaze to her father. "Mr. Pastel, I want you to close the shop during the investigation."

"This is ridiculous. So it means my daughter and I are prisoners in our own shop."

"I don't want any arguments. The point is … you are ALIVE."

Detective Fuji then pointed his mobile at a set of the footprints and snapped a photograph, then walked to the door, flipped the "Open" sign over so it read "Closed," smiled reassuringly, and said, "I'll be in touch. Stay safe."

"Oh, Father, what about my studies? I have to attend college. I can't just…"

"Let's go in the kitchen and fix a warm meal, then think about what we can do afterwards."

Before long, police guards were standing outside. Henry and Bertha decided to get some sleep.

****

The following morning, at the Police Station, a bony middle-aged lady entered barefoot and looked around. Her body was covered with tattoos, and she wore a dark blue cloak with red skulls over it.

A police lady approached her. "Yes, what can I do for you?"

"I must speak with Detective Fuji."

"What's it regarding?" She inspected the woman from head to toe.

"The murders. You could say I'm a witness."

Just then, Detective Fuji appeared. He was relishing a vegan burger with some French Fries. "Please come into my office er…"

"I'm a high priestess, but you may call me Madam Xoozi Hara, pronounced with a 'Z'."

"Follow me, please."

Once inside, he asked her to be seated, but she declined and sat cross-legged and closed her eyes.

"Please, Madam Xoozi Hara, make yourself comfortable."

She smiled, inhaled deeply, then rose midway in the air and opened her eyes. Detective Fuji dropped his lunch on the floor and stood gaping in disbelief.

"Oh, I know. You must be one of those magicians. Hah, you ought to be on a talent show. Anyway, please tell me what you know about the murders."

"He cannot die. He is already dead."

*"What?!"*

"Duppy is not a mortal. He's an apparition. You can never stop him … ever." For a moment, her eyeballs turned gold, then back to hazel brown again.

"Enough of your tricks, Madam Xoozi. You're wasting valuable police time. There's a sick, twisted maniac, a serial killer out there, and you're performing magical feats in my office. Please leave."

Her eyes filled with rage. "Foolish man. You think I am bluffing. I will prove to you that I am real. Now, focus your mind on your left leg, which is paralysed."

She stared at it and chanted some mantra in an ancient language. Then reached out both her arms. Electric sparks fired at it, then stopped.

"Now, can you feel the sensation in it?"

Detective Fuji placed his hands over it and pressed. His face lit up and he smiled in ecstasy.

"You … you cured it." He stood up and moved around on the floor like a young man.

"Thank you so much. Please forgive me."

She smirked and made her way to the door.

"Madam Xoozi, you said you witnessed something. Can you help me in my investigation? We have to stop this serial killer … Dubby."

"Do not mock the dark ones! He is known as Duppy, an apparition. He is a spirit and can appear and disappear as he pleases."

"You seem to know a lot about him. How come?"

"That's because it's my misfortune that he is my child." She snapped her fingers and vanished.

"What?"

The door burst open, and a police officer entered, trying to catch his breath and spoke, "Lieutenant, there's been another Maze Murder, and … all the police guards have been killed."

"What about the girl and her father?"

"They're safe."

"All right, let's go."

It was late evening when they arrived at the *Maze of Phantom Spectres*. Detective Fuji was horrified at the sight before him.

Not only were there butchered body parts, but foul words were carved on them with a knife.

He felt sick and vomited. Then his eyes lit up.

"Of course. I need to talk to whoever's running this place, the owner." The only problem was that the Funhouse Theme Park was so massive, and he did not have a map. The place was closed to the public, so there was no one he could ask. He clenched his left fist.

"Damn it. Who owns this place!?"

There was a crackling sound, like an electric current, and Madam Xoozi appeared without warning and sat cross-legged, floating in the air.

"If you *must* know, then this place belongs to my son … Duppy! And now that you *do* know, you must prepare to die.

"Oh, Duppy dear! Your din-din's ready. Come and eat before it gets cold!"

Before Detective Fuji could respond, the ground under his feet trembled, and two decayed arms ripped through the earth. The pale, bony hands clutched his legs with a grip of steel and pulled him down into the ground.

Silence followed. Unlike the previous murders, this one was clean and silent, and no one would ever know. Duppy was now free to come out and kill again or perhaps wait until next Halloween.

What fun that would be!

## The End?

# *Under a Dark Moon's Horn*
## *by*
## *Marge Simon*

Jenna arranges a set of Edwardian chairs side by side on the beach, one red, one brown. I smile, for she wears her best bombazine blouse, giving us a hint of the night's festivities ahead.

We bleed ourselves under the dark moon's horn. Jenna's fluted silver dipper shines with our fluids, as smiling, she ladles our offerings into the tureen. Once a communal bowl, it is again so.

Later, when the moon lowers in the southern skies, she summons her warriors to drink. We do enjoy those moments, waiting for another war to manifest itself, if not in the worlds beyond our door, then here. Yes, here on this silver beach, as the goddess known as Jenna plays her cello, Bach's Suite Number Two in D Minor, and the soldiers dance around her, mad with lust.

### *The End*

## The Last Great Hunter by Matthew Wilson

How soft and low she sings there
The survivor of her murdered tribe
Who howls at the moon's beauty
As her hunter's fail to try and hide.

Unwisely they dared into the woods
Where yellowed eyed wolves will sleep
To take the treasures they guarded
Till guilt in my mind did start to creep.

I wept at the bloodied fur we left
But now I think I am the last
Cold with only jewels to warm me
Regretting many ventures past.

Now the moon is praised with music
And I know that she is near
The wolf who will end my guilt
For murdering her loves most dear.

# Transfer
## by
## Christopher T. Dabrowski

"Oh, my God," Stanley mumbled, woken up by the pressure in his chest.

He felt he was struggling to breathe.

*Oh, Mother, my heart is failing,* he thought, terrified. Sighing for the last time, he passed away. At the same time, a fly above his head died also. There were a lot of flies in Stanley's house, although it was difficult to define the place as a real home.

He used to live in a tiny room with a kitchen. If you came into the house, you would be surprised by the dust everywhere. If your eyes got used to the semidarkness of the place, your nose would be attacked by the unidentified stench of spew, spilled alcohol, and the remains of moldy food scattered around the room corners.

After a few moments, you would see an unbelievable shamble when you could look around at last. There were many empty vodka, beer, and wine called "TUR – strength and power" bottles on the floor. Moreover, there was mold on the walls, just between the layers of peeling paint. On the untidy bed, there was grey dirt, probably bed linen. Filthy dishes piled up in the sink like Kilimanjaro Mountain. Some broken plates littered the floors; they were the ones that couldn't stay on the movable Kilimanjaro construction.

However, we are not watching a programme about interior design. Let's move our attention to the fly which passed away and has stayed on the unmovable Stanley's chest. She was killed because of the deadly concentration of alcohol in the air—our protagonist, as you can conclude, was an alcoholic.

He was now on the bed with a wide-open mouth, a mouth with remains of teeth which would lead each dentist to a heart attack.

He was looking far away with his blind eyes. *Far away* means ceiling in the physical world. However, the surprise in his eyes suggested that he saw something completely different at the point of his death. The stained-with-something navy blue beret moved from his balding and graying head. In that condition, Stanley will be found by social workers in a week. They will be called by the neighbor, who regained his consciousness after his next dose of alcohol.

As the author of the story, I have moved too quickly, leaving the protagonist behind. Dear, in reality, Stanley hasn't died. At least, not completely … let's move back to the past a little bit. At the moment, a fly, not being aware of anything, was flying directly into Stanley—he was a source of different tastes for the fly—our protagonist felt that all his pain disappeared. He experienced a blissful state, just like after drinking a bottle of alcohol. He became aware of the ceiling full of water stains and cracks, which suddenly … was torn apart like a sheet of paper.

"Oh, Beelzebub! What's that?" he shouted.

Meanwhile, Beelzebub finished his job, and Stanley noticed a wave of lights through the hole.

*Am I having hallucinations or what?* He wondered.

Suddenly, he perceived luminous hands emerging from the hole. He was captured with powerful strength and pulled up toward the dazzling light.

He was doubtlessly resting on something. But what was that … it was not defined. Neither hard nor soft – strange in a way.

His eyes got used to his new life situation at last. The first thing he saw was a huge, tomato-red face. Neither male nor female, but one thing was sure—it wasn't a gob of a policeman who was inviting him to the intoxication ward. It also wasn't a gob of a supervisor employed in this same place. It was a good and, at the same time … terribly bored face.

"Welcome! You have just died, and you are in Heaven," the stranger mumbled in a monotonous voice as if he were reciting a poem learnt by rote.

Stanley became numb and couldn't say a word.

"I'm an angel. My name is Armuel."

The speaker stood upright. He didn't look like an angel; therefore, Stanley concluded that he must have passed out drunk and hit his head into something hard. He was probably lying drunk on the floor in a supermarket, and "the angel" was a staff jester.

"You!" He got nervous at the thought of being the centre of fun.

The young guy, looking like a supermarket staff person, shook his head and stood upright. Stanley noticed wings on his back.

*Hitched, attached … but it is no reason to make fun of me!* He got irritated.

Stanley was ready to fight in defence of his drunken honour. He jumped to his (spiritual) feet. It resulted in two somersaults and landing on his belly on the floor.

"You, karate fighter, take it easy!" He panted. "Do you want to break my bones?"

*Appearances are misleading,* he thought. *He seemed to have such a nice face. He is like a snake in the grass.*

Silent, Armuel crouched in front of Stanley, which caused his wings to open. His eyes were like cocker-spaniel ones.

They were silent for a while, looking at each other, and at last, the angel concluded that the first shock had passed. *Newly dead always make trouble in their new way of life after the grave.*

"You can't make sudden movements because you see how it ends," the angel told him. "Take into account the fact that now you are using your astral body."

Stanley had no idea what the guy was talking about, but after experiencing the brutal power demonstration, he preferred to follow this winged madman's orders.

"Continue lying down, as I have to explain everything to you," the angel mumbled.

Meantime, a beautiful naked woman passed behind the angel's back.

"Ooooh…" Stanley smacked his lips lewdly.

"Oh, it's only another model. She was on a diet for too long." The angel waved his hand carelessly, as he didn't need to use his eyes to see.

He perceived everything without using his senses. The eyes, like also his body, were only a mockup of ectoplasm. He needed them to avoid scaring his patients, as he called the people under his charge.

The angel waited for some time, being sure that his "patient" would be quiet for a moment, and he started again. "You are here only for a few minutes. We will analyze your deeds and see what you could merit in your future life. I know, maybe you don't like to be here…."

Drunkard Stanley, satisfied with the view of the naked woman, concluded that he liked to be here.

"… but if you obey my rules, everything will go smoothly, and you will be born anew without being aware of the fact."

"Born anew…" Stanley repeated the words thoughtlessly, but in his dreams, he was touching all the curvy parts of the woman's body, though in her case, it would be more appropriate to use the word "bony."

The angel realized that his speech made no more sense, and he stood up carefully.

Stanley regained consciousness and looked around, trying to find the woman. He couldn't find her anywhere, but he made out the shadow of another busty woman. He tried to catch the dreamlike beauty, but the ground became too slippery, almost like soapsuds. He would have "kissed" the ground again if it hadn't been for Armuel's quick reaction; he managed to grab him at the last moment.

Sobering up, Stanley stole a glance at his saviour. "Thanks, guy," he muttered.

"You see, you should have listened to me," the angel replied.

Stanley glanced around wildly. He found himself in what looked like a supermarket. All the shelves were filled with boxes in different colours. There were plenty of packages, and the interior of the supermarket was full of motley.

Armuel understood that "newcomers" often behave like nosy children, so he continued his speech – just like a policeman who is cuffing a prisoner and has to read him his rights, although he is not listened at all.

"As you already know, you have died, and you are in Heaven, precisely speaking, on Heaven's porch because Heaven is an enormous club on floor 190034567858. You have yet to be at this level because to get there, you will have to come back to Earth and improve your *kharma*."

"Oh, guy, what *kharma*[1] are you talking about? Am I a pig or what? Do you want to turn me to flesh and then slaughter me? Speak to me like a human, or I will slap your face." Stanley sighed. He much preferred to check the contents of the boxes instead of listening to this big-headed blockhead.

"Eh, I feel like drinking a pint of beer." *A nice cold beer,* he imagined.

"Okay, let's start anew." Armuel tried again. "You have to make your soul perfect to become pure love."

"Sure," the soul of the drunkard grunted, reaching for the first box.

"Improvement of the concentration of mind through meditation at 0.003% - only ten points!" the light green caption contrasting with the crimson label said.

"Fucking shit." He put the product back on the shelf.

"As an alcoholic, you scored many points, but you need about a hundred or thousand or even more incarnations to become a VIP and get a pass," Armuel continued.

"Of course, it depends only on you whether it is going to be a hundred or thousands of incarnations. And your way, maybe a better one, starts here. Now you can make your crucial decisions relevant for your future incarnation, taking into account your points."

"Points?" Stanley got excited, putting back the next, in his opinion, useless box and assured greater commitment in a passionate prayer.

"Yeah, and if you want, you can start by watching a film about your life in our cinema. The performance is not expensive and will help you make wiser decisions."

"You, my dear friend, do you have *Deep Throat?*"

"Me?" The angel became stunned. "I am only a spirit; what you perceive is only bodily illusion."

"Fucking hell, I mean the film title…."

"Aaa, no. We here only…."

"And what about *Aliens 8* or *Constipation?*"

"Nope. You don't want…."

"I don't," Stanley told him.

"As you wish," the dauntless angel replied.

"Your loss, you barmy," he added, feeling disgusted for this primitive dope. *Why do I have to work with such goofs? Eh, it is my fault…*

Armuel had known subordination while working on Earth as a spirit companion. In his opinion, it was the shittiest job he could have; however, it appeared that the job in "Heaven – Your Paradise" was much more tedious and GOOFY!

Armuel was downgraded for organizing regular trips to the material world because he felt like indulging in human pleasures. He managed to do it because he took control over human bodies – precisely speaking, he possessed humans. He had already been a policeman and a priest. Unfortunately, his first few visits were really shocking. When he was in a human body for the first time, he was really shaken. Then he took control of a red-haired boy on a bus. The trip finished with flogging by one of the passengers, and the boy ended up with a broken nose. However, practice makes perfect, so his last visits to the earth ended with wild parties involving something humans called alcohol and drugs, including the most pleasant entertainment, which is SEX. It was something for which he envied people the most. He was envious of sex initially, but later, in heavenly monotony, his memories blurred. In the beginning, he was able to understand human sexual desires. Later on, he became more and more irritated with them. Heavenly boredom decerebrates.

**** 

"It's time for you to decide whether you want to be a man or a woman," Armuel told Stanley.

Out of anger, Stanley dropped "Vegetarianism Tendency – Only One Hundred Points."

"What, me as a woman? What are you talking about, you barmy? I am and I will be a man!"

"There is a discount when you decide to change your sex," the angel whispered. "But it is your decision."

Armuel intended to mention that in one out of a hundred cases, somebody who is born as a man and was a woman in the previous life may still feel like a woman and vice versa – but if this dill gave up at the beginning, interrupting him in the course of each sentence, it was his business. At least one idiot less.

"So, let's go! Your score is 57598, so I will take you to floor fifty-five thousand and a half."

"Hey, mister, would it be possible to exchange my score for a supply of alcohol for my whole life?"

"Nope! The alcohol floor is just below the club over there, very, very high. It is intended for VIPs."

Stanley pulled a face as if he sipped an alcohol-free drink by mistake. "Okay, I am following you."

The angel snapped his fingers, and everything around Stanley changed.

The shelves vanished, and instead of them appeared a group of containers filled with human bodies.

A voice chattered from an invisible loudspeaker. It was as if somebody had placed a parrot in front of the microphone at a railway station.

"Flo – oor fii – ftyyy fiii – veee thooo- usaaa – ndddd and a haa- lfff!"

"Oh, God, it sounds like Wayne[2] speaking in a hoarse voice." Stanley pulled his face, mentioning his buddy who smoked three packets of strong fags without a filter every single day.

"Let's turn right," Armuel said. "All the bodies represent human beings in their prime of life. There's a label under each of them. I am going to sit down for a while, and meantime, you look at them and choose one for your next life. If you have any questions, call me and I will appear immediately."

Stanley's soul gave the angel a black look and moved forward to look at the bodies.

**** 

As soon as the airhead disappeared, Armuel blew on the floor, and it became covered with soft cushions.

*At last, time for some sweet laziness.* He smiled and placed himself on the pillows. *A tired worker is a bad worker!*

He was resting and recalling good times when they celebrated with Meheb, the devil-aristocrat. Devils are fallen angels – so dreadful that they cannot work with the clients intended for a heavenly place. They were picking up women. They were tasting alcohol of the highest standard.

*What a wonderful period of time it was.* He yawned.

His spiritual eyelids were becoming heavier and heavier.

*The problem with the boozer was solved. A few hours will pass before he finds a body.* The angel smiled. *So maybe it is time to have a nap, hmm?*

He did as he had thought.

Armuel fell asleep blissfully. He had a wonderful dream: he possessed a rock star just before he started a concert in a giant stadium. Of course, he wouldn't act like himself if he didn't have a bally idea, despite the fact that he was an angel. The rock star intended to initiate the concert with his standard song, "The Number of the Beast," but the angel decided instead to make this body sing "Marian Litany" with his clear alto. Unfortunately, he didn't follow through with his idea because he was woken by a strong kick in his side. The semiconscious angel opened one eye, then the other, yawned, and sat up, unaware of what was happening.

"What is going on here, comrade Armuel?"

"What, who?" fretted Armuel.

Koscislaw Pluszak, section commander in General Affairs of the Astral Department of Ward Heaven, recited like an automation. Blushing, he yelled: "ATTENTION!"

The terrified angel leapt up, realizing who he was dealing with. He stood erect and tense while Pluszak stared at him with a malicious smile, twirling his long mustache around his finger.

"So! You idle away your time while on duty? Yes?"

"Yes, Section Commander! I report that I was idling away my time while on duty!" Armuel shouted. He preferred to be obedient and not to deny Koscislaw. He didn't want to be degraded in the angel hierarchy, as he was afraid of being transformed into a devil and sent to Hell. He would be really lucky if he was allowed to escort evildoers' souls. However, in the beginning, he'd become a typical devil who was responsible for general order. It meant that, just like damned souls who are locked in the astral cages, he would have to listen Marian Radio Station[3] all the time.

Armuel had to admit that the board members must've been really bright because listening to this radio station was a devilish torture.

"Good, very good," Koscislaw murmured, then roared, "It means, fuck, not very good!"

Armuel tried not to look at Pluszak's bloody eyes, but avoiding his bad breath was impossible. He remained silent, as it felt it was the best solution. *Let the bloke yell and vent his frustration. He'll calm down and turn a blind eye.*

He wasn't mistaken. The bloke shouted for another five minutes, calling him a devilish person who discredited the Virgin Mary and a dope unworthy of licking the devil's toilet bowl. Finally, he shut up.

"Fuck, I hope it is the last time."

"Yes, of course, the last time," Armuel shouted and was grateful to Providence that this time, he managed to avoid problems again.

"And now, forward march! Work your ass off for the client."

"Of course. I will work my ass off for the client," Armuel replied. He ran to Stanley, who was like an angel to him at that moment.

**\*\*\*\***

"On duty!" hollered the still-stressed angel.

"What?" Stanley muttered. His words were like honey for the bee.

"I am just checking to see if you need anything. Maybe you have some questions?"

The boozer scratched himself, let out a tuneful fart which assured that his astral bowels were functioning well, and said, "These bodies are so … defective!"

"What?" asked Armuel in disgust.

"Let's take this one. It says he is clever and creative, but it doesn't say how much alcohol he can sip. Is his liver in good condition? It doesn't say. Heh, it doesn't even say how strong his head is. All of this is shit here!"

Disgusted, the angel scratched himself in the place where hair should be, but he did not show off his astral bowels. "You know, for the models on this floor, we haven't provided any addictions. They have special safety devices."

"Eeee, I don't want them!"

*What am I to do with this nut?* The angel started losing control. "Okay, if you don't want to … let's move to the thirteenth floor."

He snapped his fingers, and they moved to a similar room. The difference was that the containers' contents weren't the same, thankfully for Stanley. The drunkard brightened up and moved his flashlight toward the containers. He saw a street tramp. The boozy red veins were visible on his skin and looked like a city plan with detailed roads. His eyes were also bloody, as if he suffered from insomnia. He had a dull smile. A carelessly placed fag was visible from between his only two teeth. A glazed cloth covered his head. Several greasy strands of hair were falling onto his forehead in different directions.

The picture was familiar to Stanley. He used to see a similar image daily in his filthy mirror.

He looked at the label:

"Predisposition to alcoholism as well as to smoking. He will probably be addicted to sex and alcohol. Life expectancy is much above the average. Intelligence level below average."

The list was extremely long, but Stanley was fed up with reading. He preferred to ask this winged dope.

"Hey, you. Will I be able to hump if I am him?"

"Not so much. You will become impotent because of drinking alcohol and smoking."

"And is it possible to buy one with potential? Because it is so cheap." He pointed at the model.

"Of course, we are having a lot of discounted models on sale."

"Does he have a strong head for alcohol?" asked Stanley.

"Yeah, he does, but his liver will be damaged soon."

"I would nourish it, wouldn't I?"

"Of course, as you wish," the angel replied. "We can add body immunity against alcohol's effects. The price is also reduced."

Stanley kept asking about other different package deals, then went shopping. He bought another package deal: "Personal Charm – only 2000 points." It was supposed to influence women. He then came back to the chosen body.

"It's not the best choice," the angel told him.

"It's not your business! Do you want me to mace your face?"

"I am only informing you, in case you want to change your mind."

"Zip up your face at last! I want it and that's it." Stanley got really irritated.

"Okay, fine! But remember, you will still have your free will. Despite these parameters, you will still have a chance to turn out a successful man."

"You, angel, stop bulling me! Let's sail through it."

"So, adieu!" The angel sighed and snapped his fingers. "I wish you a sweet and lovely life."

In the next instant, Stanley found himself in a strange red tunnel with a light at the end of it. He was moving towards the light faster and faster, remembering less and less about himself. At last, his head was empty of thought. He was thrown into the light with enormous power.

****

A newborn child started crying.

"Ooooh, Jesus!" murmured a drunken Michayla.[4] "Wayne! Come here! You will cut my umbilical cord."

"Coming, coming!" semiconscious Wayne muttered. He had difficulty speaking as he smoked three packs of fags without filters daily…

## *The End*

[1]*Kharma* is pronounced in the same way as *karma* which in Polish means a food for animals.
[2]A random name used by the translator as the original Polish name Wiesiek does not exist in the English list of names.
[3]*Marian Radio Station* - is a Polish religious, conservative, anti-post-Communist and pro-life Roman Catholic radio station and media group, describing itself as patriotic. It was founded in Toruń, Poland, on December 9, 1991 and run since its inception by the Redemptorist Tadeusz Rydzyk, often called Father Director by his followers. The station has been criticized by both Polish and international media, notably for perceived misconceived patriotism, the use of Catholicism as a political tool. (Wikipedia: http://en.wikipedia.org/wiki/Radio_Maryja)
[4]A random name used by the translator as the original Polish name Mieczyslawa does not exist in the English list of names.

# Haiku by Denny E. Marshall

Spirit forms in room<br>
"Ghost of Christmas?" You ask<br>
"No, the Grim Reaper."

©2018 George E. Marshall

# *About the Contributors*

**Linda Barrett:**

Ms. Barrett has been writing all her life. She wrote her first book at the age of eight. It's still in the McKinley Elementary school library. She was published in the *Huntingdon Junior Library* literary magazine by age thirteen. She's won three awards with the Montgomery County Community College Writer's contest. "Mr. Cat's Revenge" won third place in the 2014 MCCC contest. Ms. Barrett lives with her 84 years young mother in Abington in the same house for 50 years."

**Sharon Bidwell:**

Sharon Bidwell is a multi-genre writer who had her first published short story described as having 'both a Sci-fi and horror element, strong on characterisation and quite literary, in terms of style'. She loves to create this brand of Dark Fiction, most commonly seen to date in her short stories. Longer works most notably include *Space: 1899*, the Lethbridge-Stewart series, and a short audio story for Doctor Who. She lives in the south-west of England writing dark, gritty, and even outright twisted tales. She's lived in a house with a Harry Potter cupboard under the stairs, shared a publisher with the creator of Roger Rabbit, and once took a trip to Jupiter. Only one of these has been in her imagination. http://www.sharonbidwell.co.uk

**Rajeev Bhargava:**

Rajeev lives in Harrow with his parents and five Chihuahuas. He has been writing since the age of twelve but had his first work published in 1990. Since then he's been writing stories, poems and articles for the small press as well as mainstream. His ambition is to be a freelance writer.

**Alexis Child:**

Alexis Child hails from Toronto, Canada, home to dreams and nightmares. She worked at a Call Crisis Center befriending demons of the mind that roam freely amongst her writings. Alexis once lived with a Calico-cat child sleuthing all that went bump in the night and is haunted by the memory of her cat. She is currently working on her second poetry collection and starving in the garret with her muse. A starving child is a frightful sight. A starving vampire is even worse. Please donate nonperishable food items and B-negative blood (and make it a double!).

Alexis Child's fiction has been featured in *Danse Macabre, Schlock, Screams of Terror,* and UK's *Dark of Night Magazine*. Her poetry has been featured in numerous online and print publications, including *Aphelion, Black Petals, Blood Moon Rising Magazine, The Horror Zine, The Sirens Call,* and elsewhere. Her first collection of poetry, *Devil in the Clock,* a dark and sinister slice of the macabre, is now available on Amazon.

Visit her website: http://www.angelfire.com/poetry/alexischild/; Alexis's YouTube Channel: https://www.youtube.com/channel/UCg6S5u4yX73kA1ZWGnKaEBA/videos

**Christopher T. Dabrowski:**

Christopher has had numerous books published in the USA and Poland. His USA works include: *Anomaly* and *Escape*, both published by the Royal Hawaiian Press. Books published in Poland include *Anima Vilis* (Initium), *Grobbing* (Novae Res), *Deathbirth and other Stories* (Agharta & Amoryka), *Orgazmokalipsa* (Alternatywne publishing house), *Anomalia* (Forma publishing house), and *Ucieczka* (2017 - Dom Horroru publishing house). Monika Olasek provided the English translation for his *Night to Dawn* stories.

**Sandy DeLuca:**

Sandy has written five novels; *Settling in Nazareth* (she painted the cover art), *Descent, Manhattan Grimoire, From Ashes,* and *Requiem for the Dead*. Her poetry chapbook, *Burial Plot in Sagittarius* (also created cover art and illustrations), was nominated for the BRAM STOKER award in 2001. Her art has been exhibited in galleries, hair salons, book stores and online venues. She has also painted covers and contributed interior illustrations for various numerous small press venues.

**Chris Friend:**

Chris has published his art in small press horror magazines for nearly 25 years. His surreal horror images have been featured in *Stygian Articles, Realm of the Vampire, Deathrealm, Black Petals,* and *Space and Time.* He draws his inspiration from Harry Clarke, H. R. Giger, and the horror comics of the 70s such as the Tomb of Dracula her and the Hammer Studios Frankenstein films. Chris friend can be reached at Mars_art_13@yahoo.com. Chris friend can be reached at Mars_art_13@yahoo.com.

To sample his illustrations, go to http://chris.michaelherring.net and http://www.moonlit-path.com/art-2-13-06.htm.

**Todd Hanks:**

The creative writing of Todd Hanks has been seen in publications such as Asimov's Science Fiction Magazine and the Kansas City Star newspaper.

**Tom Johnson:**

Tom, a Vietnam veteran with twenty years in the military police (L.E.), has enjoyed literary success as a science fiction novelist with his action adventures in the Jurassic Period of Earth's predawn. He has created short story SF characters like Captain Danger of the *Space Rangers* and the galactic master thief, *The Forever Man* as futuristic space opera adventure. His many costumed crime fighters include two of his own creations, such as *The Black Ghost* and *The Masked Avenger,* as well as a western masked hero of the plains called *The Nightwind.* He has upcoming stories of *Ki-Gor the Jungle Lord,* and Greek heroes like Hercules and Atalanta. For the latest information on Tom and his writing, check out his websites:

http://www15.brinkster.com/jur1/index.html
www.geocities.com/fadingshadows1/index.html.

**Hal Kempka:**

Hal's stories have been published in numerous magazines and ezines including *Night to Dawn, Blood Moon Rising, Black Petals, Inner Sins, Sanitarium, Yellow Mama,* and *Microhorror.* His horror short fiction anthologies, *Blue Plate Special* and *Discarded Treasures,* are currently available on Amazon Kindle, Barnes and Noble, and Smashwords, among others. *Discarded Treasures* is available in both paperback and e-book. Other anthologies including his stories are Pill Hill Press: *Zombie Art Inspired Short Stories, Blood Bound Books: Seasons in the Abyss,* and Post Mortem Press: *Shadowplay.*

**Hillary Lyon:**

With an MA in English Literature from SMU, Hillary Lyon founded and for 20 years served as senior editor for the independent poetry publisher, Subsynchronous Press. Her speculative, horror, and sci-fi stories have appeared in numerous print and online publications. She's also an illustrator for horror/sci-fi, and pulp fiction sites. And she loves to hand-paint furniture and accessories.

**Rod Marsden:**

Rod Marsden hails from Sydney, Australia. He has three degrees related to writing and history. His stories have been published in Australia, England, Russia, the USA and now Canada. He has work in the American anthology *Cats Do it Better,* the American steam punkanthology *Break Time* and in the Canadian anthology *Morbid Metamorphosis.* Many of his short stories have been published in *Night to Dawn* magazine. His books include *Undead Reb Down Under and Other Vampire Stories, Disco Evil: Dead Man's Stand, Ghost Dance,* and *Desk Job* (his salute to Lewis Carroll). *Cold Water Conscience* is his venture into Crime/Horror. His short play, *Zombie Vision,* was well received at Cronulla Arts Theatre. His play *Hyde and Seek* was even better received. Rod has a fondness for Cronulla and the Wollongong area but an abiding love for the more northern Clarence River region of his home state of New South Wales.

# Denny E. Marshall:

Denny E. Marshall has had art, poetry, and fiction published. Some recent credits include interior art in *Midnight Echo* #14 Dec. 2019, cover art for *Society Of Misfit Stories* Feb. 2020, and poetry in *Space &*

*Time Magazine #134* Fall 2019. This year his website is celebrating 20 years on the web. Also in 2020 his artwork is for sale for the first time. It is available on Zazzle as posters coffee cups, puzzles, mouse pads, etc. The link is on his website. (Click on top left drawing.) See more at www.dennymarshall.com.

**Elizabeth Hattie Pierce-Collins:**

Elizabeth first learned art and drawing from her mother. From there, she was self-taught until she was able to attend art school. She loves drawing the human figure and never stops studying the human body in motion. Her illustrations have appeared in *Night to Dawn* magazine and *The Spider's Web* (a novel). These have drawn positive attention from the readers. Elizabeth hopes to appear in more magazines and books in the future. For more information, contact Elizabeth at wackyursalinan45@aol.com.

**Marc Shapiro:**

Marc has been a busy beaver. His story *Let Me Take You Down* was printed in book form in the Short Sharp Shocks imprint of Demain Publishing on December 31. Upcoming from Demain is his debut poetry collection *Existential Jibber Jabber*. Already out: his unauthorized biography of Keanu Reeves entitled *Keanu Reeves Excellent Adventure* (Riverdale Avenue Books) and the shortest story he's ever written, four sentences under 100 words, on the website Warp 10 Lit. Marc Shapiro has a very patient and understanding wife.

**Marge Simon:**

Marge Simon's works appear in publications such as DailySF Magazine, Pedestal, Dreams& Nightmares. She edits a column for the HWA Newsletter, "Blood & Spades: Poets of the Dark Side," and serves as Chair of the Board of Trustees. She won the Strange Horizons Readers Choice Award, 2010, and the SFPA's Dwarf Stars Award, 2012. She has won three Bram Stoker Awards ® for Superior Work in Poetry, two first place Rhysling Awards and the Grand Master Award from the SF Poetry Association, 2015. In addition to her poetry, she has published two prose collections: *Christina's World*, Sam's Dot Publications, 2008 and *Like Birds in the Rain*, Sam's Dot, 2007. Her poems appear in *Qualia Nous* (Written Backwards), *The Dark Phantastique* (Jasunni Productions), Spectral Realms anthologies by S.T. Joshi, and more poems will appear in *Chiral Mad 3* and *Scary Out There*, a HWA/ Simon & Schuster Y/A collection, 2015. www.margesimon.com

**Ann Stolinsky:**

Ann's most phenomenal publishing credit is a story published in March 2020 in *Klarissa Dreams Redux,* a charity anthology that has been selected to go to the moon in a time capsule with an organization called Writers on the Moon (https://www.writersonthemoon.com/how-it-works).

Her most recent publishing credit is a short story in *Galaxy #7*, by Clarendon House. A short story was published in *Bananthology* in 2021 by HDWP Press. A poem was published in *Poetica 2* in December 2020 by Clarendon House. Several of her short stories appear in other Clarendon House anthologies, Sweetycat Press anthologies, and have been published by Gallery of Curiosities, and *Tales from the Canyons of the Dead*, among others. A poem was published in the Fall 2015 issue of *Space & Time Magazine*. Ann is a member of the Writers Coffeehouse in Willow Grove, PA, and a writing critique group.

Ann Stolinsky also is a partner in Gemini Wordsmiths LLC, a full-service copyediting and content-creating company. www.geminiwordsmiths.com

Gemini Wordsmiths formed a publishing imprint, Celestial Echo Press, www.celestialecho-press.com, in May 2019. Their first anthology, *The Twofer Compendium*, was published in December 2019. Their second, *The Trench Coat Chronicles*, was published in December 2020. In 2021, Celestial Echo Press published *TIME Blinked*, a novel written by George W. Young. In 2022, they published *DracuLAND*, a novel also written by George W. Young.

**Matthew Wilson:**

Matthew Wilson has had over 150 appearances in such places as *Horror Zine, Star\*Line, Spellbound, Illumen, Apokrupha Press, Gaslight Press, Sorcerers Signal* and many more. He is currently editing his first novel and can be contacted on twitter @matthew94544267.

**Lee Clark Zumpe:**

Lee Clark Zumpe has been writing and publishing horror, dark fantasy and speculative fiction since the late 1990s. His short stories and poetry have appeared in a variety of publications such as *Weird Tales, Space and Time* and *Dark Wisdom;* and in anthologies such as *Dark Horizons, Best New Zombie Tales Vol. 3, Dread Shadows in Paradise, Heroes of Red Hook* and *World War Cthulhu*. His work has earned several honorable mentions in *The Year's Best Fantasy and Horror* collections.

An entertainment columnist with Tampa Bay Newspapers, Lee has penned hundreds of film, theater and book reviews and has interviewed novelists as well as music industry icons such as Paddy Moloney of The Chieftains and Alan Parsons. His work for TBN has been recognized repeatedly by the Florida Press Association, including a first-place award for criticism in the 2013 Better Weekly Newspaper Contest.

Made in the USA
Middletown, DE
21 July 2023